Love Street

By Andrew Matthews

RED FOX

A Red Fox Book

Published by Random House Children's Books
20 Vauxhall Bridge Road, London SW1V 2SA

A division of The Random House Group Ltd
London Melbourne Sydney Auckland
Johannesburg and agencies throughout the world

3 5 7 9 10 8 6 4 2

First published in Great Britain by
Red Fox Children's Books in 2000

Printed and bound in Great Britain by
Cox & Wyman, Reading, Berkshire

Papers used by Random House Group Ltd are natural,
recyclable products made from wood grown in sustainable forests.
The manufacturing processes conform to the
environmental regulations of the country of origins.

The Random House Group Limited Reg. No. 954009

www.randomhouse.co.uk

ISBN 0 09 940337 4

For Gemma
with love

ME STUFF

*Pru drove her little open-topped sportscar down
Love Street, her red hair streaming behind her. She
smiled as she remembered the moment at the office
lunch when Mr Maddox, the editor of the* Wongalloo Herald *had stood up and said, 'Now it
gives me great pleasure to present the award for
Young Reporter of the Year to . . . Pru Delaney!'*

*Pru had been totally overcome, not knowing
whether to be embarrassed or overjoyed, and the
only words she had been able to find as she accepted
the award were, 'Thank you', but everybody had
applauded, and seemed happy for her.*

*The award, a golden pencil embedded in a block
of blue perspex, was propped up beside her on the
passenger's seat. Pru wondered how her house-
mates would react to the news. Josie was bound to
make a fuss and want to celebrate – any excuse
to party; Shaylene would pretend to be pleased, but
inside she would be jealous. Shaylene hated it when
someone else was in the spotlight.*

*Pru turned into the drive of Number Fifty-Two
and got out of the car. Her neighbours, the
Hoppers, were in their front garden. Barry was
watering the lawn, Fiona was taking cuttings from*

a shrub. *Barry grinned and waved when he saw Pru. 'G'day!' he called out. 'You're full of smiles.'*

'Why shouldn't I be smiling?' said Pru. 'That's what people do when they're happy, isn't it?'

Barry laughed his teddy bear laugh, but as Pru shut the front door behind her, his face became thoughtful. 'You know, Fi,' he said, 'when I think of all that girl's been through, it makes my business worries seem pretty damned trivial.'

'I know what you mean, Baz.'

'Difficult to think that it's only two years since her parents were tragically killed in an auto wreck that almost cost her her life.'

'It certainly is,' said Fiona. 'She's gone from strength to strength.'

Barry nodded, his distinguished grey hair shining silver in the sun. 'What beats me is why a young, bright, beautiful girl like that doesn't have a queue of fellers lined up outside her door.'

Fiona snipped a shoot with her secateurs. 'Pru's a shy girl,' she said. 'Mind you, the two she's sharing with don't help. They pounce on any likely-looking young males. I reckon Pru would do better for herself if Shaylene and Josie moved out.'

Barry turned off the hose and said, 'Fi, there's something I've been meaning to tell you. I should have said something before, but . . .'

'What is it, Baz?'

'Old Doc Tucker called me into the surgery on Monday. He wanted to have a word with me about that blood test I had done.'

'Oh?'

2

Barry's lips were thin. 'Apparently, there's something not quite right about my blood count,' he said grimly. *'I've got an appointment to see a specialist.'*

The music went – Tunk tinka tunk, tinka tunk, tinka tunk *– and a girl's voice sang:*

On Love Street the smiles never end,
On Love Street everybody's your friend,
On Love Street they're willing to share
Your tears and your laughter, your joy
and despair,
On Love Street wherever you go,
You get what you need just by saying hello
To the people you know,
On Love Street.

And then my mum walked in. She did a double take, blinking at me, like: What on earth are you doing, Suzanne? She said, 'What on earth are you doing, Suzanne?'

'Watching telly,' I said.

Mum started blinking really fast. 'Watching telly?' she said.

'Yes.'

'But it's not switched on.'

Good point.

'Oops!'

I blame John Keats. He's a Famous Dea~~d~~ Person who wrote a poem about autumn – know the one than goes on about *mi mellow fruitfulness?* Anyway, I was in Year Nine and Mrs Parker's English class, and it was autumn, so she made us read the poem. Outside, autumn was nothing like the way John Keats described it; it was grey and drizzly, like the start of a really depressing old black and white movie. I didn't want to be in school, or English, and I didn't want to be reading a poem by John Keats or anybody else – I didn't even particularly want to be me.

So I flipped, freaked; whatever. By which I mean, my imagination went: *No, no, can't handle this at all!* – and whisked me away to *Love Street* for the first time. I saw the bay, the café, people sunning themselves on the beach, hunks and babes splashing one another; then Love Street itself, whitewashed bungalows with tiled roofs, neat front lawns, bougainvillea flowering like Flamenco dancers' skirts. People came out of the houses in couples and families. They smiled and waved to each other, and the title song started: *On Love Street, the smiles never end* . . .

Mrs Parker said, 'Suzanne?'

I said, 'Sorry, miss?'

'The line *Where are the songs of Spring?*' said Mrs Parker. 'What do you think Keats means when he asks that question?'

I said, 'I expect he's wondering where the songs that were sung in Spring have gone.'

This didn't go down at all well.

4

I'm here to tell you, Famous Dead People are a menace.

After that, *Love Street* turned into a game; kind of. Like if I was wound up, or worried – I worry a lot – or just bored, I'd slip away to *Love Street* to see what was happening. It was generally more interesting than what was going on in my own life. And don't get me wrong, I'm not a basket case, but even though I knew I was making it all up in my imagination, it felt like it was making itself up, and I was just watching it. On a TV screen that wasn't there. Well, it *was* there, but I was the only person who could see it.

Love Street became a habit, and then an addiction. It came by itself, usually when I ought to have been doing something else, and sometimes when I *definitely* didn't want it to – like in the middle of a conversation or something.

OK, yeah, it wasn't normal, but plenty of people do stupider things – and it was completely and totally harmless.

You have some kind of problem with that?

2

MUM AND DAD STUFF

Oh yeah, the Parentals. Complicated. No question that life would be a lot easier if you didn't have to have parents. Everybody has complications with their mums and dads, right? But I'll swap you mine for yours, any day.

It goes like this: Pat (Mum) married Patrick, then found out he was carrying on with Diane, who was married to Bob. Pat divorced Patrick, Bob divorced Diane, who married Patrick. So then Pat and Bob started seeing each other, fell in love, got married and had me. (That means Bob is Dad – got it so far?) But then, when I was four, Pat found out that Bob was carrying on with Julia, who wasn't married to anybody, until Pat and Bob got a divorce, when she (Julia) married Bob and had Timothy, my half-brother.

I don't remember a lot of arguments happening at the time, just the sad feeling in the house, and Mum bursting into tears all over the place. For years she couldn't get the hang of cooking for two, and served me with massive portions at mealtimes, which probably had a lot to do with my weight problem.

This is where the complication starts: Dad lives in York, which is two hundred-odd miles away. I see him whenever I want, and even when I don't want, because Mum likes to get shot of me every once in a while, which I think is fair enough. In theory. Dad rings at least once a week to talk to me, and when he's finished doing that, he talks to Mum. They're supposed to be friends, rational and civilised with no hard feelings, but they row like they're still married.

And Dad still tries to come the Heavy Parent with me.

Like just before my birthday. Dad's on the phone, giving it: sorry I can't be there on the day, work, Julie, Timothy and blah. He says, 'Planning on doing anything special?'

I say, 'I've got tickets to see this tap-dance group in Guildford, they're supposed to be excellent.'

Dad says, 'I thought your mother couldn't stand tap-dancing?'

I say, 'Oh, Mum's not going. I'm going with some mates from school.'

Dad says, 'But their parents are going with you, surely?'

'No.'

'You mean to tell me that your mother's letting you go on your own to Guildford, at night?'

I say, 'Dad, I'm not going on my own, I told you. I'm going with some mates.'

And suddenly it's my dad, the pit bull terrier. He says, 'Put your mother on.'

Ten minutes of trench warfare. I can't hear what Dad's saying, but I can hear the way he's saying it, and it's not pretty.

Mum splutters, goes red, says, 'I'm not behaving irresponsibly, I'm—! Suzanne is perfectly capable of—! But she's been to Guild—! What drug-crazed gangs? What are you—?'

It ends, like most of my parents' conversations, with Mum slamming the phone down as she shouts, 'Impossible! Im-bloody-possible!'

I wait a couple of minutes for her to re-enter Earth's atmosphere, then I say, 'He's a paranoid, interfering control-freak.'

Mum's really touchy about how I feel towards Dad, so she starts apologising for him. 'He can't help it,' she says. 'He feels guilty that he's not the father he wanted to be. He still feels responsible for you. You're still his daughter, when all's said and done.'

I say, 'Sure, but he's still a paranoid, interfering, control-freak.'

Mum looks at me like I don't understand; *she's* the one who doesn't understand.

Being a single parent isn't easy, as Mum is always pointing out. I agree. The only thing worse than being a single parent, is being a single parent's daughter. You know how some

8

people neglect their kids, shoot them money and leave them to get up to whatever they want? Sometimes I feel I could hack a bit of neglect like that.

Mum and Dad are afraid that because they got divorced, I'll grow up to be twisted, or turn into a right tart, or run amok with an axe, so they overcompensate. All I actually do is school work, homework, and as I'm told. Mostly.

I keep telling Mum, 'Lighten up, will you? I'm going to be all right. One day I'll meet a nice man, settle down and make you into a granny.'

Mum looks relieved when I say things like this, and gives me one of her must-be-doing-something-right smiles.

She is *so* gullible.

3

MEMORY STUFF

I'm on GCSE Study Leave, and right now I'm supposed to be revising French verbs, but I'm not. For one thing, I know them, so there doesn't seem a whole lot of point, and for another, every time I look at my text book and notes, my mind goes back to last year. Weird, but there are days when it feels like a long time ago, and days when it feels like last week. You ever noticed that time is the wrong way round? Like, when you're in a dentist's chair having a scrape and polish done, half an hour is forever – but when something good's happening, two hours can go – *Dwip*!

It started with the auditions for the school production. Nattie, Jan and I were . . .

No, hang on! It was before that, when . . .

Hmm! Memory stuff is tricky, isn't it? You *think* you can remember things straight, but when you try, everything gets tangled up like an old bit of string.

French verbs are easier, even the irregular ones.

When I was in Year Ten my life was a tragedy.

I don't mean earthquakes, raging fire or the World colliding with a comet the size of Denmark – just your average, everyday kind of tragedy.

Myself, for example. I knew I wasn't drop-dead gorgeous, but I hoped I was attractive in a creep-up-on-you way, so that a boy who knew me but hadn't paid me much attention would suddenly go: 'Hey! I've never noticed before, but Suze Finch is attractive. I think I'll ask her out.'

Unfortunately, the mirror said: pale, soapy-green eyes, short mousy hair, rabbity overbite and freckles. Most of all, I used to hate the freckles; I thought they made me look six years old. When people who liked me were having a good day, they told me my freckles were cute; people who didn't like me called me 'Dotty' behind my back.

So, from the neck up was a disaster, and from there on down it got worse. I used to have what Mum called 'a weight problem', which was a nice way of saying that I was Miss Wobbly Chops. When I was in the Juniors and Year Seven, my sensitive and considerate class-mates only referred to this every ten seconds or so. I dieted, went jogging, dancing and tram-polining, slimmed-down, and by the time I was fourteen I wasn't chubby any more, and I knew I had excellent legs, because I was in the school library one lunchtime, and I overheard these two boys in my registration group – Robin

11

Usher and Martin Scott – talking about me on the other side of a set of shelves.

Robin said, 'Suze Finch got excellent legs, ain't she?'

I thought, 'Don't say – *Shame about the freckles*. Please don't say – *Shame about the freckles*.'

And Martin said, 'Yeah. Shame about the freckles.'

The problem was, I was convinced that there was a fat girl inside me just waiting to burst loose and balloon. On bad days, I looked at myself in the mirror and I could *see* the weight going back on: my chin trebling, my bum cheeks expanding, and I thought, 'No one's ever going to ask you out.'

And I only had bad days.

Sad, yeah? I was Juliet without Romeo, Jane Eyre without Mr Rochester, Olive Oyl without Popeye.

Tragedy!

And then there was Beth. There *had* to be Beth, just to show me that when Life has it in for you, it goes all the way.

Beth was my best mate, and had been since Infants. I liked her the first time I saw her, and she liked me when she found out that I could do the work she didn't understand. I was – *Smile, smile! Let me help you with the answer! Be my friend!* Beth was – *Take, take, take!*

Somewhere in the middle of Year Seven,

Beth started to turn into a Babe – and I'm talking heart-shaped face, slim straight nose, moonlight hair, summer-sky eyes. Boys turned their heads when she walked past; *girls* turned their heads as she walked past, and wanted to top themselves because they didn't look like her. At fourteen, if Beth wiggled her little finger, it was wall-to-wall testosterone.

And did this make her happy? Get real! Nothing made Beth happy: boys, school, parents, birthdays, Christmas – she moaned about everything, constantly and at great length. To me. Well, that's what best mates are for, aren't they? You ring them up and drone on for hours about how unfair everything is because your mum and dad give you every-thing you want, and all the best-looking boys in your year keep asking you to go out with them.

For instance: Beth and I had just spent our last day in Year Nine, and were walking home from school together. I'd got that tra-la-la feeling about the holidays starting, and it being weeks before I'd have to say, 'Oh no!' when I woke up in the morning.

Beth said, 'Guess what my dad's done! Go on, you'll never guess.'

I said, 'What's your dad done?'

Beth wrinkled up her nose. 'Only gone and booked a holiday in Florida, hasn't he? He wants to take me and Mum to Disney World.'

13

I said, 'But, Beth . . . you've always wanted to go to Disney World.'

'Yeah,' said Beth, 'but Dad didn't bother to ask me about it, did he? He said he wanted it to be a surprise. Now I'm going to have to buy loads of new clothes, and it'll take me ages to find a pair of sunglasses that suit me.'

I said, 'But, Beth . . .!'

'And we're not staying in a hotel,' said Beth. 'Not good enough for Dad! He's rented this big house, with a pool. TV in every bedroom, with cable and satellite.'

I said, 'But, Beth . . .!'

Beth said, 'Everything has to be perfect with Dad. Even a holiday. Everybody has to have a good time. Sickening, isn't it?'

So, when I was fourteen, I had a non-happening love life, a best mate it was impossible to do anything right for, and I was obsessed with an Australian soap opera that didn't exist.

Cool, or what?

4

TONY STUFF

When Tony Beckwith joined Cressfield Comp at the start of Year Ten, it was a major hormonal event. Tony was tall, had curly black hair, huge brown eyes, a great lop-sided smile and tight buns. He wasn't handsome, exactly, but the *way* he wasn't handsome made girls keel over and froth.

Beth spotted him first. We were doing our break time walk, up the side of the tennis-courts as far as the library, and then back down again. Not the world's most interesting walk, but a good way of avoiding collisions with Year Seven brats.

Beth was eating a bag of crisps, and she said, 'These crisps don't taste as good as they used to.'

I said, 'Don't they?'

'They're all chemically. Nothing like smoky bacon.'

'No?'

'Crisps are really bad for you, anyway. They're fattening, and they give you zits.'

None of this, you understand, actually

stopped Beth from eating the crisps. It sounded like she had a mouthful of broken lightbulbs.

'A raw carrot would be much healthier,' she said.

I had this vision of an Orange Revolution at Cressfield Comp: every kid in school bombing out at break, pulling carrots from their pockets and munching on them – fifteen hundred Bugs Bunnies.

'It'll never catch on,' I said.

'What?'

'Raw carrots. They haven't got the oomph of crisps and Mars bars.'

Beth raised one eyebrow, as she always did when I said something she didn't get, which was frequently. 'Oomph?' she said.

I said, 'People don't want healthy stuff at break. They want to pig out on chocolate and junk food that makes them feel like they've really indulged themselves. It's comfort-eating. My theory is . . .'

I was big on theories, but Beth wasn't listening. She was standing with her mouth open, eyes boggling, still as a Pointer who's caught a scent. Her voice went into slow-motion: 'WHO – IS – THAT?'

I turned, and saw Tony by the tennis-court gate. He looked embarrassed, because these two Year Eight girls were coming-on to him. They were jiggling about like a pair of kittens in a paper bag.

16

My stomach went down a water slide; it was lust at first sight.

Beth, too. Her eyes were going – DEE-DOO! DEE-DOO! DEE-DOO! – and her tongue was practically hanging out.

My Super-Suze data base flashed into action, and I said, 'Must be the new guy in Ten Green West that everybody's been going on about. He looks a bit—'

'He looks very,' said Beth. She was: radar locked onto target, all systems, fire! She said, 'Is he going out with anybody?'

I said, 'He only arrived yesterday!'

'S-o!' said Beth. 'He's not going out with anybody!' She seemed to have made up her mind that he soon would be.

I said, 'What about Gary?'

Gary was Beth's latest. Over the summer, she'd gradually prised him away from Yasmin Khan, and I'd been battered with all the details. Beth cried on my shoulder so much that my T-shirts shrank, and I'd had plenty of ear-sweats from long telephone calls.

Natch, as soon as Beth got Gary, she started to lose interest. She would have looked good in Hunting Pink and a black velvet riding-hat.

Beth said, 'Gary Marlow is *boring*!'

So, poor old Gary was for the heave-ho. 'Oh well,' I thought. 'There are plenty of girls waiting with dustpans and brushes to sweep up the bits.' I felt more sorry for the new guy, because Beth was obviously interested in him, and Beth Always Got Her Man.

I looked at Tony again, and imagined his face on a WANTED poster. Tasty, but gut-wrenchingly, heart-achingly, tragically not for me. He was right out of my league. Like, if we were the last two people on Earth, he'd be in love with a tree.

After break, GCSE English with Mr Wright. (Mum always told me to wait until he came along. Ho, ho, ho! Quick, put me onto a resuscitator!) Beth was in Miss Peters' set, so I went to the lesson with Nattie.

Nattie's sweet – small, with bubbly hair and a bubbly personality to match. People think I talk a lot until they meet Nattie. The trick is to ignore half of what she says.

I said, 'I saw that new bloke at break.'

Nattie said, 'Is he the good-looking one? He's supposed to be Welsh, isn't he? Marianne told me. That he was Welsh, I mean. It was Becca who told me he was good-looking. Or was it Gayle? No, it was definitely Becca, because . . .'

My brain left, worked-out with weights, ran round the campus twice and got back in time to hear Nattie say, 'So, is he?'

'What – Welsh, or good-looking?'

'Good-looking. I mean, no one's going to care if he's Welsh or not, are they? Although I suppose some people might. People who don't like Welsh people would, wouldn't they?'

I said, 'He's a hunk. His bum scores nine-point-five on the Suzanne Scale.'

So, into English, on the front row with Nattie and two empty chairs. In came Mr Wright . . . and Tony was with him.

The class fell silent. The air was filled with the sound of yearning females. I think I heard a sigh – or it could have been a moan.

Mr Wright said, 'This is Tony. He's joining our set. Treat him kindly, it's his first day, and it's not easy coming into a big school like this . . .'

Especially when a teacher stands you in front of a group of twenty-eight strangers and talks about you. Tony handled it well, nods and uncertain smiles.

' . . . but I'm sure it won't take him long to settle in,' said Mr Wright. 'Find a seat, Tony, and I'll take the register.'

My heart went BOMP-A-BOMP-A-BOMP because the only available places were the two next to me and Nattie.

Tony walked over, plonked himself on the chair beside mine, turned to me, grinned and said, 'Hello, there.'

He had a lovely, singing Welsh accent that made, 'Hello,' come out as, 'Hulloo'.

I was goo. My face ignited. I said, 'H-!' and it was all I could manage.

Couldn't tell you what the lesson was about;

19

didn't hear a word. I was concentrating on sending out feminine vibes, hoping my attractive-so-it-creeps-up-on-you would leap, instead of creeping.

And it worked, sort of, because when the bell went, Tony leant over to me and said, 'Excuse me, but I wonder if you could help me? I'm a bit lost. I've got History next, in E26, and I don't know where it is.'

I said, 'Out the door, turn right, first door on your left, up the stairs and E26 is straight ahead.'

Tony gave me another liquefying grin and said, 'Thanks a lot. My name's—'

'Tony,' I said. 'I'm Suze, short for Suzanne.'

'And I'm Nattie,' Nattie chipped in. 'Short for Natalie. I only get called Nattie at school, because my mother doesn't like it. When I get called Nattie, I mean, not the school.'

Tony's eyes clouded over – a common phenomenon among people who talked to Nattie. 'I'll remember,' he said. 'Thanks again, Suze.'

'Anytime,' I said. In my mind, I added, 'Anything, anywhere!'

Nattie and I watched Tony leave, and Nattie's eyes were: DOH! She said, 'Hmm, well, yes, ah! She was right, then.'

'Who was?'

'Marianne,' said Nattie. 'She said he was Welsh.'

I thought, 'Somewhere, sometime, there'll

20

be hope for you, Nattie – but not this planet and not this incarnation.'

I didn't say anything, because Nattie was a mate.

Beth and I met up at lunchtime in the Sandwich Room. I told her Tony had sat next to me and spoken to me, and her eyebrow went: DOYNG!

'What do you mean, he *talked* to you?' she said.

I said, 'You know, mouth opens, words come out.'

'But what did he want to talk to *you* about?' said Beth.

I thought, 'Oh-oh!' because there was definitely a hint of green in Beth's clear blue eyes. Like, how come Tony talked to someone like me when there was someone like her about? And, get this: *I thought she was right!*

I said, 'Oh, nothing. Just hello. I think he's shy.'

'Shy, eh?' said Beth. She was like a cat at a mouse-hole.

That's when Jan appeared: Jan of the glossy black hair, pine-forest green eyes, Pocahontas cheekbones and legs up to her armpits; Beth's only serious competition in Year Ten. Jan staggered over to the table and said, 'Oh, my God! Oh, my God! I've just seen *the* most *gorgeous* boy! I think I'm in love! In fact, I *am* in love!'

I said, 'Is his name Tony?'

Jan said, 'You know him? Where did you meet him? Where's he from? Got his phone number?'

Beth narrowed her eyes, and I knew there was going to be trouble in the not-too-distant future, and right there and then I went:

Pru walked into the lounge to pick up her car keys, and found Shaylene and Josie standing at the window. Shaylene was wearing her powder blue shower robe, her shiny, healthy, newly-washed hair reaching almost to her waist. Josie was wearing a white T-shirt and denim shorts that showed off her long, shapely legs. Her dark hair moved like a curtain as she half-turned her head when Pru came in.

Pru said, 'What's got you two so interested?'

'The new neighbour at Number Forty-Eight,' said Josie. 'Come and check it out.'

Pru moved across the room to the window. A furniture-removal wagon was parked across the road, and two men in overalls were lifting a sofa out of it, anxiously supervised by a young man in his early twenties. The young man was tall and broad-shouldered, with black hair and a striking face, sensitive and finely-chiselled.

Josie said, 'Now he's what I call a real spunk.'

'Who is he?' said Pru.

'No idea,' said Josie. 'But I intend to find out as soon as possible.'

'Not if I find out first,' Shaylene murmured.

Something about the tone of Shaylene's voice

made Pru look at her. The blonde was staring fixedly at the young man across the road, and her eyes were like a hungry tiger's.

Tunk tinka tunk, tinka tunk, tinka tunk . . .

5

UNDERSTANDING STUFF

I nearly dropped the phone. My voice went squeaky. 'Me?' I said.

'Well, you know the guy,' said Beth.

'I spoke like five words to him at the end of English! We're not exactly bosom buddies.'

'Look, it's easy,' Beth said. 'We've got English next door to each other tomorrow afternoon, yeah?'

'And?'

'I'll get out of the lesson as soon as I can and wait for you in the corridor. If I'm not there, keep him talking until I turn up, then you can introduce us.'

'Why can't you introduce yourself?'

'Because he might think I'm after him or something.'

I said, 'But, Beth, you *are* after him!'

'Yeah, but I don't want him to know that, do I? He might think I'm being pushy.'

I thought, 'I wonder how many teenagers are having conversations like this, right this second? If life was straightforward, the phone companies would go out of business.' I said, 'I don't know, Beth. This feels a bit sneaky.

Wouldn't it be better to wait until after you finish with Gary?'

'I already did,' said Beth.

'When?'

'Soon as I got in from school.'

I said, 'Don't you think it might be better to wait for a week? If Gary sees you talking to Tony, he's going to feel—'

'A week?' said Beth. 'You saw what Jan was like today. If I don't do something fast, she'll be in there.'

'But Jan's going out with Dominic. They've been together for three months.'

Beth snorted. 'Jan's not going to let Dominic stop her, is she?' she said. 'You know what she's like.'

I thought, 'Yes, she's just like you.'

Beth put on her hard-done-by voice. 'I thought you were my best mate, Suze. Best mates are supposed to help each other out, aren't they?'

I knew what would happen if I said no: sulks, sighs, silences, bitchy remarks. Beth was going to emotionally blackmail me into it sooner or later. I decided it might as well be sooner. 'All right,' I said.

'Great!' said Beth.

Not, 'Thank you, you're a real friend, what would I do without you?' – just, 'Great!'

After I put down the phone, Mum came into the hall holding up her watch. 'Twenty-five minutes, thirty-seven seconds,' she said.

I said, 'Beth rang *me*. It's not our phone bill.'

Mum said, 'You spend hours on the phone and *I'm* the one who pays for it. How does that make it *our* phone bill? And you've been at school with Beth all day. You walked home with her three hours ago. What's happened since then that took her twenty-five minutes, thirty-seven seconds to tell you about?'

I said, 'Boy stuff.'

'I wish you'd spend less time sorting out Beth and her boyfriends,' said Mum. 'It might give you more of a chance to find a boyfriend of your own.'

'There are loads of boys I'd like to go out with!' I said. 'They'd just rather go out with Beth, that's all.'

Mum sighed and shook her head. 'And whose fault is that?' she said.

I wasn't sure what she meant. 'Beth can't help being better-looking than me, it's not like she does it deliberately.'

'You'll learn!' said Mum.

'Learn what?'

'There's no point in my telling you. You have to find out for yourself.'

Don't you just hate it when adults do that to you – like they know something you don't, but they won't let on what it is? Sometimes I think they're conning us, and that really they don't know any more about anything than we do.

★

26

Homework: Maths, Biology, reading through Act One Scene One of *Romeo and Juliet*, wondering why anyone would *want* to bite their thumb, leave alone find it insulting, wondering why a famous love story should start with a bunch of yobbos duffing one another up.

I vaguely registered the doorbell going, the sound of voices; then Mum called up the stairs, 'Suzanne! Someone to see you.'

I thought, 'Beth? Nattie? Jan? A double-glazing salesman?'

Wrong! I got to the front door, and Gary was standing in the porch.

I had a thing about Gary Marlow, dating back to Year Nine. He had chestnut-brown hair, twinkly grey eyes, to-die-for long lashes and a dazzling smile. I'd found it ironic that I'd helped Beth get it together with him, when I wanted to get together with him myself – so ironic that I'd cried about it in the privacy of my bedroom.

'This is it!' I thought. 'Beth's spell has been broken! Gary's realised that I'm warm, loyal, sensitive, loving and busting to snog him! It's finally going to happen!'

But one look at Gary's face told me that it wasn't. His eyes were red from crying, and his shoulders were hunched in pain. 'Hi, Suze,' he said. 'I was wondering if you fancied a stroll and a bit of a chat.'

I said, 'Beth?'

27

Gary smiled like he'd been found out. 'Um, yeah,' he said.

I ducked my head round the lounge door. 'Just going out for a walk, Mum,' I said. 'Won't be long.'

'He's rather nice,' Mum said hopefully.

'Beth's ex,' I said.

Mum groaned.

We left the house and walked down the street towards Gosport Road. Gary was awkward, ducking his head like he was dodging punches, not sure how to start. 'Sorry about just turning up like that,' he said. 'Only . . .'

'You needed someone to talk to,' I said.

'Yeah! And, well, you've always been easy to talk to. You understand stuff, and – '

'I'm Beth's best mate.'

'Mm.'

I said, 'Look, Gary, if you're hoping I can get Beth to change her mind, then I'm sorry but – '

'I know,' Gary said.

'Then what *do* you want to talk to me about?'

'I want to know why she finished with me. Last week we were . . . and now we're . . . What did I do wrong?'

It was sad. Gary was in the school football team, County Junior Cross-Country Champion, brilliant swimmer, all-round good guy – and here he was, as forlorn as an abandoned spaniel, and I didn't have the faintest idea what to do about it, and I went:

Pru and Rod strolled barefoot along the damp sand above the tideline at Wongalloo Bay. Rod's handsome face looked careworn, and there were dark circles underneath his swimming-pool blue eyes. They stopped at a big, flat-topped rock and Pru sat down, hugging her knees as she gazed at the pink and gold sunset.

Rod picked up a pebble from the sand, rolled it over between his fingers and then flung it towards the incoming waves. 'I couldn't get my head around it for a while,' he said. 'I thought Shaylene and I were really close, you know? Then she dumps me, just like that.'

Pru said, 'I don't know why she did it, Rod. Shaylene keeps herself to herself. She doesn't talk to me about personal stuff much.'

'It's down to me, isn't it?' said Rod. 'I've taken a good, hard look at myself, and I realise that I was an idiot to fall for her in the first place. I must be the world's biggest loser, right?'

Pru blinked at him, her eyes wide with concern. 'You mustn't think that way,' she said. 'Sure, it didn't work out between you and Shaylene, but that doesn't mean there's anything wrong with you.'

Rod laughed bitterly. 'But that's the whole point, Pru,' he said. 'There is something wrong with me. I was blind. I was so wrapped-up with Shaylene, I

29

couldn't see that the right girl for me was right under my nose the whole time.'

'She was?'

'Yes,' said Rod. 'And now that I'm seeing clearly, I can only hope that it's not too late for me to do something I should have done a long time ago.'

Pru frowned. 'What are you saying, Rod?' she said.

Tunk tinka tunk, tinka tunk, tinka tunk . . .

'You didn't do anything wrong,' I said.

'Then why . . .?'

I could have told Gary the truth. I could have said, 'Because Beth is a completely selfish bitch, who's dumped you because she's seen someone she thinks she'll look better with. She's taken her bite out of you, now she's thrown you over her shoulder and she's reaching for the next peach in the fruit bowl.'

But it would have hurt him if I had, and I was too considerate to do that.

I said, 'She was afraid that you cared more about her than she did about you. She thinks you're both too young to get serious. She feels really bad about finishing with you, but she was afraid it would hurt more if she left it any longer.' It was just a hotchpotch of things I'd read, and seen on TV and at the cinema, but I was really cooking. I said, 'Sometimes, when two people get together, one starts to try and change the other, so that in the end that person

30

is completely different from the person that person was when the relationship began. Beth cared too much about you to do that to you.'

Gary said, 'So . . . she finished with me because she cares about me?'

'Maybe when you're both older,' I said.

I was trying out lines from *Love Street* in real life. I hoped that if a boy ever finished with me, he'd let me down as easily.

Gary said, 'Yeah, maybe. Thanks, Suze. Pity Beth couldn't have explained it like that.'

'What did she say?'

'Not a lot. She told me she didn't want to go out with me any more, put the phone down and wouldn't answer when I rang back.'

Subtlety was never Beth's strong point. She was more the hit-them-over-the-head-and-chuck-them-in-the-river type.

'Give it time,' I said.

'I will,' said Gary. 'Well, better be heading back, I suppose.'

'You don't have to. We could talk some more if you want. Not about Beth – anything you like. It might help you take your mind off things.'

'No. I think I'd rather be on my own for a bit.'

'You can talk to me any time,' I said. 'Really. Give me a buzz, or just come round. We could go out somewhere.'

'Thanks for the offer, Suze. You're pretty OK, you know?'

OK for whitewashing Beth's dirty work, OK for spreading ointment on bruised male egos – but not OK for going out with.

Sad person with no life, right?

Following afternoon, English.

The bell goes for the end of the lesson, Tony stands up and walks out.

I get up like someone's dropped an ice cube down my knickers.

Nattie says, 'Hang on, Suze!'

I say, 'Sorry!' and rush outside. No Beth – argh! Tony's walking down the corridor in a thick stream of pupils on their way home.

I shout, 'Tony!'

Everybody looks at me. I want to shrivel up and die.

Tony stops, turns, sees me and gives me a puzzled smile.

I battle my way through the crowd. When I reach him, he says, 'Suze?'

I say, 'I was, er, just, sort of, wondering how you were getting on, kind of thing?'

'Fine,' says Tony. 'Everybody's really friendly.'

'They are, aren't they?' I say. 'It's a really friendly school, isn't it? Even the kids who go to it think it's really friendly.'

God, I'm sounding like Nattie!

'Yes, it is,' says Tony.

I say, 'And what do you think of *Romeo and Juliet* so far?'

Tony says, 'Suze, are you trying to ask me something?'

'No, no! I, er, found the first scene a bit tricky, you know, and ... talking to other people about things sometimes helps you to get them straight, doesn't it?'

I'm waving my arms about, shifting my weight from foot to foot like I need the loo, or I'm about to break into a song and dance routine.

By now, Tony is convinced I'm bonkers, and is starting to worry that I might be dangerously bonkers. His eyes go CLICK! CLICK! as he glances from side to side to find an escape route.

Beth sidles up to me. She's brushed her hair, and is all fluttering lashes and lip-gloss. She says, 'Well hi, Suze!'

I say, 'Hi, Beth.' I'm so relieved to see her that I forget I'm supposed to be introducing them; then I remember as Beth's eyebrow goes up. 'Oh, sorry,' I say. 'This is my friend Beth. This is Tony.'

Beth says, 'Hi, Tony. You're new, aren't you?'

I've seen the look on Tony's face before. It happens when boys meet Beth: their jaws go slack and whirlpools start spinning in their eyes. Tony's having his first Beth experience, and it's like falling down a lift shaft. He tries to say something: 'I-er-um-ah . . . H-hello, Beth.'

Beth gathers what's left of him in her hands, and melts it with a smile.

This is love going on; this is what Shakespeare and all those famous poets wrote about – and I helped it to happen.

I'm so jealous, I want to scream.

6

DATING STUFF

Beth transformed herself into a cross between a Field Marshal and Sherlock Holmes. Via the grapevine and detailed personal observation, she learnt Tony's routine: his mum dropped him off at school at eight-fifteen, and after last lesson he waited in the library until he was picked up at three forty-five.

Beth went into action. She browbeat her dad into driving her to school so she could be in time to say, 'Oh, hi, Tony! So you come to school early too? How amazing! What a coincidence!' At the end of the day, she developed a sudden compulsion to do homework in the library – 'You again! Funny how we keep running into each other, isn't it?'

Operation Tony meant that Beth and I didn't see a lot of each other. Even at break and lunchtimes, if she spotted Tony anywhere near, she left me in mid-conversation and bore down on him with all-the-better-to-eat-you eyes. She never apologised to me for this. We were such old friends that she knew I'd understand. Or, to put it another way, she took me for granted and didn't give a toss about my feelings.

Actually, I didn't mind, because it was good to get away from Beth for a while. I walked to and from school with Nattie, which was interesting. Nattie had a different take on life from most people, so you could never predict where a talk with her might end up.

For example: on the second morning we walked to school together, Nattie said, 'I could be wrong – in fact I probably *am* wrong, I usually am – but I've got a sneaky feeling that Beth quite fancies Tony.'

'Really?' I said.

Nattie said, 'D'you think they might start going out together?'

'Tony's got no choice,' I said. 'Beth's made up her mind.'

'Oh,' said Nattie.

One word – from *Nattie?* I looked at her. 'What's wrong?' I said.

'Nothing! Absolutely nothing. There's nothing wrong at all. Not in the slightest. Well, there is one tiny little thing, but it doesn't *really* matter.'

'And?'

'I wish Tony would ask me out!' Nattie wailed. 'I wish *someone* would ask me out!'

'Welcome to the club, Nat.'

'What *you?*' said Nattie, sounding surprised. 'There must be loads of boys who fancy you.'

'Must there?'

'Yes,' said Nattie. 'I mean, you're so . . . so . . .'

36

I thought, 'Pretty? Witty? Intelligent? Vivacious?'

' . . . you!' said Nattie.

'Thanks, Nat, but I have to be me. I can't help myself, and I know because I've tried. Girls who look like me get ignored. It's the girls who look like Beth that pull all the blokes.'

'She doesn't deserve them though, does she?' said Nattie, then her eyes boggled as she realised what she'd said. 'Ooh, don't tell Beth that, will you? I wouldn't like her to think—'

I said, 'Don't worry, Nat. As a matter of fact, I agree with you.'

'But you're her best friend!'

'That doesn't mean I can't see her faults.'

'And her good points.'

'Sure!'

Nattie waited four paces before she said, 'And what *are* Beth's good points?'

I said, 'Well, there's, um . . . er . . .'

'Y-e-s?' said Nattie, and she gave me this look that made us both laugh so hard that we had to lean together to keep from falling over.

That's when I discovered that underneath Nattie's clueless, motor-mouth front, lurked a dead wicked sense of humour.

Don't think I was a Beth-free zone though, because my house was still on the phone – despite Mum's threats. Every night, I got the latest thrilling instalment of *Tony and Beth: The Dream Grows*.

37

Beth said, 'He nearly held my hand today.'

I said, 'Beth, how can someone *nearly* hold your hand?'

'I could tell he was thinking about doing it, because I was thinking about it too.'

'So why didn't you?'

Beth heaved a God-she-knows-nothing sigh, and said, 'We haven't been out on a date yet. You don't hold hands before the first date. Which is where you come in.'

Sudden vision of me standing between Tony and Beth, holding hands with both of them. I said, 'Huh?'

Beth said, 'You ask Tony if he wants to ask me out and, if he does, tell me so that I can tell you to tell him it's all right for him to ask me to go to the cinema with him on Saturday.'

It took a few seconds for me to get my head around that lot. I said, 'Why can't *you* tell him it's OK for him to ask you out? Come to think of it, why don't you ask him out yourself?'

'Because he might not want to ask me out yet,' said Beth. 'If he tells you he doesn't, and then you tell me, it'll be all right – but if I ask him and he tells me himself, that'll be it.'

'It?'

'He'll go round telling everybody I asked him out and he said no, won't he? I don't want everybody to know I've been wasting my time on a boy who doesn't want to go out with me, do I?'

I said, 'Ah! So you think he *doesn't* want to go out with you?'

'No,' said Beth, 'I'm sure he does, but you've got to tell him it's all right, otherwise he might not be sure enough to ask.'

She'd lost me.

You know that place where parallel lines meet, and chimps type out *Hamlet*? That's where Beth's thinking makes sense.

Next day, I had English just before lunch. At the end of the lesson, I was all psyched-up to talk to Tony, but he beat me to it by saying, 'Suze, d'you mind if I ask you about something?'

I said, 'Go right ahead.'

Tony glanced at Nattie and said, 'It's a bit . . . well . . . private.'

I told Nattie I'd catch up with her in the Sandwich Room, and Tony and I walked out of the English Block, and went to sit on the brick bench outside the Technology Suite.

Tony looked serious. 'This is a bit of a cheek, I know, but I need your advice,' he said.

Good thing to say. I was like: *Dr Suze, Counsellor.*

I said, 'About what?'

'Your friend Beth. I've been thinking about asking her out, but I'm nervous.'

'You can relax,' I said. 'There's a film on at the Cineplex that she's dying to see. If you ask her to go with you, I'm sure she'll say yes.'

'That's not what I'm nervous about,' said Tony.

'Sorry?'

'I don't seem to have much luck with girls, see. Like, when I lived in Wales . . .'

Tony told me the story of himself, Rose, Sian, Lynne and Carys. They'd all gone out with him and given him the run-around, playing mind games and throwing wobblers.

Basically he was whinging, but I didn't notice. I was too busy listening to his soft Welsh voice and being gobsmacked at finding out how many girls like Beth there are in the world.

'I've had it with all that,' Tony said. 'I want a girlfriend I can talk to. Someone who's on the same wavelength as me – someone who wants me for who I am, not what I look like. So . . .'

'So?'

'If I go out with Beth, will she give me a hard time?'

Direct, hey? I puffed and spluttered like an over-filled kettle coming to the boil. 'What am I supposed to say to that?' I said. 'Beth's my friend, so I'm not going to tell you anything bad about her, am I? I know she wants to go out with you, so if you want to go out with her, do it!'

'But don't expect too much?'

I was: 'Whoa! This guy knows what questions to ask!'

'I didn't say that,' I said.

'I know,' said Tony. 'And thanks for not saying it, Suze.' He grinned. 'So who are you going out with?'

'No one.'

'*Really?*'

I wasn't sure why he said it the way he did, and I didn't think about it afterwards, because Tony had just shattered a lot of my illusions. Up until then, I'd assumed that looks were everything, and that all boys cared about was how pretty you were. Now I'd discovered that there was more to it than that, and it was disturbing. Maybe there was a whole new set of rules for me to learn – or, even worse, maybe there *weren't* any rules. Maybe people just made it up as they went along.

Saturday evening, Nattie and I were mooching about in the Cineplex foyer, waiting for our movie to be called, when Nattie said, 'There's Jan!'

And there *was* Jan, walking towards us with a smile, looking good enough to give a Supermodel an inferiority complex.

I said, 'Hi, Jan!'

Jan said, 'Hi, guys! You're not going to see *Deadly Persuader Three*, are you?'

''Fraid so!'

'Mind if I join you?'

I said, 'Why, are you on your own?'

'Uh-huh.'

'Where's Dominic?'

41

'Oh, we were getting a bit stale,' said Jan. 'We decided on a more open relationship.'

'What does that mean?'

'It means we don't have to do everything together. Like we can see other people if we want to, no pressure.'

I said, 'Whose idea was that?'

'Mine,' said Jan.

Nattie said. 'So . . . you and Dominic are still going out together, but you're not going out together?'

'Uh-hu,' said Jan.

I knew Nattie was about to give me one of her looks, and that we'd both crack-up if she did, so I turned away – just as Beth and Tony came in through the sliding doors, arm in arm.

I said, 'Well, well, well!'

Nattie said, 'What a surprise!'

Jan said, 'Just look at her, will you? She's wearing him like a new coat!'

'Make a nice couple, don't they?' said Nattie.

'He can do better than that,' said Jan. 'Much, much better!' And I went:

It was a quiet evening at The Blue Cockatoo. *Pru was seated at the bar, nursing a drink and talking to Josie, who was wearing her waitress-uniform: a navy blue top and a black mini skirt.*

'So what did Rod want?' Josie said, polishing a beer glass with a dishcloth.

'Oh, nothing. Just needed to talk,' said Pru.

42

'I thought he was hoping the two of you might get together.'

Pru lowered her eyes and a blush stole across her face. 'I'm too busy with my job for any kind of relationship,' she said. 'Anyway, I don't think Rod should get involved with someone else while he's still on the rebound from Shaylene.'

There was a burst of laughter from the other side of the room. Josie looked across and her eyes narrowed. 'Didn't take her long to get her hooks into the new neighbour, did it?' she said resentfully.

Pru turned, and saw Shaylene and Tom at the pool table. Shaylene was pretending that she didn't know how to play; Tom had his arms around her, showing her how to hold the cue.

'They look pretty happy,' Pru said.

'Yeah? How long d'you reckon that'll last?' said Josie. 'She'll get fed up with him and dump him, just like all the others.'

Pru shrugged. 'Sounds like you'll be the first in line when she does.'

'Maybe I won't wait that long,' said Josie, with a sly smile. 'Maybe I should do something about it before she dumps him.'

Tunk tinka tunk, tinka tunk, tinka tunk . . .

7

SHOES STUFF

After Beth and Tony became an item, they
dropped out of sight for a fortnight. I hung out
with Nattie and Jan. Jan was a lot of fun, but
a bit in-your-face for some people. I don't think
she deliberately tried to be the centre of attention, she was just the sort of person who got
noticed because she had such a big personality.
She was one of those people who had everything – looks, brains – and I ought to have
hated her, but I didn't.

One morning, I heard some goss in registration that I thought Jan should know about,
but I didn't tell her in school in case she got
upset. I waited until we were going home, and
Nattie was safely out of the way.

I said, 'Seen Dominic recently?'

'No,' said Jan. 'Just around.'

'Have you heard that he's going out with
Debbie Horsefield?'

Jan shrugged. 'That figures,' she said. 'He's
had the hots for her for ages.'

'Don't you mind?'

Jan said, 'You can only care about someone

so much, you know? When you come to the end of it, it's over.'

'Except for the Big One,' I said.

'What's the Big One?' said Jan.

I explained Suze's Theory of the Big One. The Big One was Real Love, True Romance, Mr Right, Your Fate-Mate, the Ideal Partner that everybody was looking for.

Jan listened, then said, 'But how d'you know when you've met him?'

'No idea,' I said. 'I think you just, like, *know.*'

'How about if you're wrong, though? Say he's your Big One, but you're not his?'

'Then he's not the real Big One. It has to be the same for both of you.'

'So it's like shoes,' said Jan.

'Is it?'

'Yeah. Going out with boys is like buying shoes, you have to try on lots of pairs until you find the ones that fit properly.'

'Right!' I said. 'The Big One is *The* Shoes!'

I suppose you had to be there for it to make sense. It helped at the time, because I stopped thinking of myself as a loser when it came to boys. I was waiting for Him: The Shoes.

Actually, a pair of carpet slippers would have been nice.

Beth was out of sight, but not out of mind, because she still phoned me every night. She had a new catch phrase: *Tony says.* Tony seemed to have something to say about lots of

45

things, and it was interesting for me to find out that, for a change, Beth was going out with somebody who could think, and not just be a mirror for her to admire herself in, or a puppet who jumped when she pulled the strings. Even so, it came as a surprise the Friday she called and said, 'What are you doing tomorrow afternoon?'

I said, 'Ten-pin bowling with Nattie and Jan – why?'

'I thought we could all do something together.'

I said, 'What about Tony?'

'Oh, Tony as well.'

'Wouldn't you two rather be on your own?' I said.

'Tony says we ought to go out more,' Beth said. 'He says he wants to get to know my friends.'

I thought, 'And it'll give you a chance to show him off in front of us.' I said, 'Sure, fine.'

And I *was* sure that it would be fine. I didn't hear the Complications Machine cranking itself up. You don't, do you? You think you're unsinkable right up to the moment when you hit the iceberg.

We met at the rink, and we had a brilliant time. Beth, Jan and I were so-so at bowling, Nattie was surprisingly good, but Tony was Tops. He was so useless that it was hilarious. He sent himself up, flapping his arms and legs around like a scarecrow in a gale, and we all laughed so much that it hurt.

That was the afternoon we invented *Person Least Likely to be Mistaken For*. You played it by picking someone, and thinking of the Famous Personality they were least like. Dumb game, sure, but it sort of brought us together, because we were the only people who knew what we were laughing about.

The togetherness went on after the bowling finished, and we all ended up round the same table at the cafeteria.

Tony said, 'This is great, isn't it?'

'What is?' said Jan.

'The five of us, being mates and having a laugh,' Tony said. 'It doesn't happen enough.'

I said, 'What doesn't?'

'Girls and boys getting together as friends, instead of girlfriends and boyfriends,' said Tony.

'That's down to boys,' said Jan. 'Boys can't be just friends. They always want to make it something more.'

Nattie and I exchanged glances, like: 'I wish!'

'I think friendship's more important,' Tony said.

This was getting pretty philosophical for a bowling-rink cafeteria, and Beth looked uncomfortable. 'Yeah, but friendship's different, isn't it?' she said.

'You don't snog your friends,' I said.

'Exactly!' said Tony. 'You snog people you

fancy, and fancying someone's not the same as liking them.'

'Isn't it?' said Beth.

Tony said, 'No. Look, there's a big difference between fancying someone, liking them and loving them.'

Nattie said, 'So you can fancy someone you don't like, and you can like someone you don't fancy?'

'Absolutely!' said Tony. 'And you can love someone you don't like. You love your parents, but you don't always like them, do you?'

Jan said, 'Well I've never met a boy who just wanted to be friends.'

'Me neither,' said Beth.

'I'd like to meet one who wants to be everything!' said Nattie.

Tony suddenly stood up, and held his hand out to Jan. 'Friends?' he said.

It was like, he was joking but he wasn't joking.

Jan frowned, then smiled and shook Tony's hand. 'Friends!' she said.

Tony did the same thing to Nattie, and then it was my turn. 'Friends?' he said.

I took his hand. It was warm, and it sent a cosy shock right through me. 'Friends,' I said.

And that was when I fell in love with him – straight out of the aeroplane door, with no parachute.

★

Jan, Nattie and I left Beth and Tony at the bus stop, and walked up Gosport Road together. I was churning inside, feeling that pang that makes you want to laugh and cry at the same time.

Nattie said, 'Tony's really nice, isn't he? Good-looking boys are usually big-headed, but he's just . . . nice.'

I said, 'He's a good guy.'

'I think Beth's dead lucky to have a boy like that,' said Nattie. 'I mean, if Tony wasn't going out with her, I wouldn't mind if he – not that he ever would, mind you – but if – '

Jan stopped walking and held her arms out straight, like someone had crucified her on the wind. 'Tony Beckwith is totally wonderful!' she said. 'I don't care who he's going out with, I love him to bits!'

'And me!' said Nattie. She and Jan looked at me.

'He's The Shoes,' I said.

Heartache is a bitch, but it's *your* bitch, so you hang onto it. On Sunday morning, I fed mine with sad records and even sadder dreams. My head wouldn't leave Tony alone. I decided to be the best friend I could be to him, because his friendship was all I could have, and that way I wouldn't feel like I was being disloyal to Beth. 'A Doomed Love that suffers in silence,' I thought, and there was something noble about the idea, and:

Pru stood on the rocks at the far end of the northern headland of Wongalloo Bay, her hair streaming in the howling wind. Waves lunged for the shore like grey bears, crashing into foam that flew into the air and speckled Pru's face. She laughed at the storm's power, and her laugh was as wild as the wind and the ocean.

A voice said, 'That's a pretty dangerous spot. I'd step back a bit if I were you.'

Pru turned and saw Tom. 'You nearly gave me a heart attack, sneaking up on me like that!' she said.

'I wasn't sneaking,' said Tom. 'I saw you from the road as I was riding past on my bike, and I thought I'd come over to warn you.'

'Thanks, but I'm all right,' said Pru.

An old grief darkened Tom's eyes. 'Yeah, reckon that's what Dezzo must have thought,' he said.

'Who's Dezzo?'

'He was my brother,' said Tom. 'We used to come fishing off these rocks when we were kids. One day Dezzo went fishing on his own, in a storm like this. He never came back. Someone saw a big wave sweep him away. It happened just about where you're standing.'

'I'm sorry!' said Pru. 'I didn't know.'

'Hey!' Tom said. 'I'm not out for sympathy. I just wouldn't like the same thing to happen to you.' He stretched out his right hand. 'Let me help you. It's getting slippery out here.'

Pru frowned, uncertain what to do.

'Come on!' said Tom. 'I'm not going to perv on you, if that's what you're worried about.'

Pru smiled and put her hand in his. She stepped forward and her trainer skidded on a patch of wet seaweed, sending her tumbling into Tom's arms.

They gazed into each other's eyes, their faces only centimetres apart.

Tunk tinka tunk, tinka tunk, tinka tunk . . .

I went down to the kitchen to help with lunch. Mum made a sauce for the chicken while I peeled potatoes, resisting the temptation to carve them into broken hearts.

'You're sighing,' said Mum.

'Am I?'

'Yes. You're in love, then.'

'Who says?'

Mum said, 'You shut yourself in your room and play gloomy records for two hours, then you come downstairs with eyes like a dead fish, and start sighing over the spuds. It's love or glandular fever.'

'It's love,' I said, 'and it's hopeless!'

'Generally is at your age.'

'Thanks, Mum,' I said. 'That makes me feel a lot better!'

'Is it anyone I know?'

'Beth's latest.'

'Not that boy who came over the other night?'

'No, that was Gary. This is Tony.'

'Gets through them at a fair rate, doesn't she?'

'It's not fair!' I said. 'When's it going to be my turn? When's somebody going to notice me, for a change?'

'When you let them,' Mum said.

8

AUDITIONS STUFF

So I'd made my mind up that Tony and I would be Just Good Friends.

But . . . how d'you do that? How can you be friends with someone who turns you into mozzarella cheese every time you look at him? How d'you keep your feelings from showing when a stampede of wildebeest is going on inside you? Friends are people you share your problems with, right? But I couldn't share my problems with Tony, because he *was* my problem.

Monday morning in registration, questions were dropping off me like bits of peeling sunburn, when Mrs Baxendale said, 'And here's a final reminder that auditions for the school production will be held in the Drama Hall after school today. Anyone interested in any part of the production should attend, or make sure that—'

I went: 'Yes! A production! Something to throw myself into! Something that'll take up so much time, I'll be able to keep my mind off my mind!'

The more I thought about it, the better the

idea got. At break, talking to Beth, Nattie and Jan, I was full of it.

Beth looked at me like I'd flipped. 'The school production?' she said. 'School productions are *boring!*'

'No they're not, they're a laugh!' I said.

'But what are *you* going to do?'

'Act.'

'*Act?*' said Beth.

I said, 'Yeah, you know – learn lines, stand on stage and say them in front of an audience? Mr Shepherd thinks I'm a good actress.'

Up went Beth's eyebrow. 'And what would he know about it?' she said.

I said, 'He's Head of Drama, Beth.'

Beth was about to go, 'Huh!' but before she could, Nattie said, 'Well I wouldn't mind getting involved. Not acting, though – make-up, or something like that.'

'And I'm going,' said Jan. 'I want to be a star!'

'Huh!' said Beth. 'It's bad enough being stuck in this dump all day, but a production means you have to stay here in the evenings as well.'

I said, 'But it's theatre! Glamour!'

Beth tossed her hair. 'You lot go ahead if you like,' she said. 'I've already got a life!'

She strode off huffily.

Nattie said, 'That girl is just all give.'

By three twenty-five, the Drama Hall was

packed with would-be luvvies and girls whose pushy mums paid for them to do evening classes at the local Dance Studio. The noise level was high enough to wreck a decibel-counter.

Mr Shepherd came in, looked slowly round, and his eyes projected beams of silence onto everybody. When the talking died away, Mr Shepherd said, 'Thank you all for coming. This year's school production is going to be *Romeo and Juliet*.'

And he told us about it while he turned and twisted, cramming handfuls of words into his mouth and spitting them out. It was an Oscar Nominations performance, and Mr Shepherd was someone you'd definitely buy a used car from. 'OK!' he said finally. 'Down to business! Those of you who want to work backstage, please sign up on the appropriate sheet in the corridor outside. Those of you who'd like to be actors, stay.'

A big kerfuffle as people squashed out through the door.

'See you,' said Nattie. She got to the door just as someone was trying to get in, going against the flow like a salmon swimming upstream through treacle. My stomach departed for regions unknown, because the salmon was Tony. 'Sorry I'm late, sir,' he said to Mr Shepherd. 'You haven't finished, have you?'

'Acting or technical?' said Mr Shepherd.

'Acting.'

'You're in luck. Take a seat.'

Tony noticed Jan and me, grinned and began to walk over to us.

'Beth isn't going to like this!' I whispered.

'Stuff Beth!' said Jan. 'Oh, hi, Tony! I didn't know you were an actor.'

Tony said, 'Well—'

'Waiting for quiet, thanks very much!' said Mr Shepherd. 'There's a lot to do, and I'd like to get through it before I die of old age. I want you to get in a circle, because we're going to warm up by doing Pass the Prop.'

Groan.

I've compared notes with people from other schools, and all Drama teachers do Pass the Prop in some form or another. You get handed a prop, and you have to stand in the middle of a circle, do a mime or say something, using the prop as anything except what it actually is, and carry on until someone gets a different idea and takes over from you. Mr Shepherd gave us an umbrella, and it became a sword, a cricket bat, a snorkel, a trombone – and then Hallo grabbed the umbrella, put the handle against the side of his head and said, 'You'll have to speak up, I've got an umbrella stuck in my ear.'

A few people laughed; I was one.

That's when I really noticed Hallo for the first time. I think it was the first time *anybody* had noticed him.

Hallo was thin – well, scrawny, to be honest – with stand-up-straight hair the colour of light shining through marmalade. He'd come into my registration group in the middle of Year Nine, after his family moved to the UK from Australia. (His dad was a computer nerd who'd landed a job with a British company.) Hallo's real name was Harold Gluck, which is why he wanted people to call him Hallo. He had a reputation for being a weirdo – mainly because he had this off-the-wall sense of humour that not many people got. I didn't know that when I noticed him at the auditions, because he was still under *Nobody* in my *Forget It* files.

Pass the Prop slowed down as everybody ran out of ideas – except Hallo. He half-opened the umbrella, stuck his head inside, and said, 'Argh, no! Death by giant fruit bat!' Then he opened it fully, rested the point on the floor and twirled round it. 'Dancing with swans!'

I'd never thought about an umbrella looking like a swan before, but Hallo made me see it. He was going to do something else, when Mr Shepherd said, 'Thanks, Harold! I'm auditioning for a play, not a one-man show.'

Hallo said, 'Sorry! Didn't mean to be a dag!' and blushed.

The blush made me feel sorry for him.

Next came readings. The boys had to do one of Romeo's speeches when he's in the orchard of Juliet's house and sees her on the balcony. The girls' speech was the bit where

Juliet winds herself up to drink the sleeping potion.

Most of the boys sounded like they were reading out a shopping list. Hallo went completely over the top, and turned the speech into a comedy sketch that made everybody laugh – including Mr Shepherd. Tony was something else. His lovely Welsh voice made the Drama Hall go still, and time slow down, and it wasn't Tony any more, it was Romeo, more in love than anybody had ever been. The performance was still hanging in the air after Tony sat down.

I gave Juliet's speech my best shot, and I thought I'd done all right until it was Jan's go. As soon as she opened her mouth, it was obvious that she was going to get the part. A few of the girls managed to show that Juliet was frightened, but Jan was the only one who managed to catch Juliet's stubborn streak, so that when she mimed swallowing the potion, it was an act of Teen Rebellion – two fingers up to Lord and Lady Capulet.

I thought, 'You rat, Jan! You have to be good at everything, don't you?'

Then it was over. Mr Shepherd said, 'Well done, everybody. Provisional cast lists will be posted at Wednesday lunchtime.'

Jan, Tony and I wandered outside.

Jan said, 'You were incredible, Suze! I don't stand a chance!'

I said, 'Jan, go home, stand in front of a

mirror, imagine I'm next to you, and ask yourself – *Which one looks like Juliet?'*

'I thought you were both outstanding,' said
Tony. 'And who was the Aussie bloke with the
hair? He was brilliant!'

'Hallo?' said Jan. 'No contest, Tony.'

I said, 'Tony, does Beth know you came to
the auditions?'

'No,' said Tony. 'I didn't mention it to her.
I don't tell her *everything*. It's not like she's my
mum, is it?'

'I don't think she's all that keen on drama,'
I said.

Tony said, 'Well, she doesn't have to come
and see the play if she doesn't want to.'

I started to wonder what would happen if
Beth *did* come to the production. How would
she react to Tony playing love scenes with Jan?
I thought, 'Beth's an intelligent person. She'll
understand that it's only acting, and that
there's no reason for her to get jealous. If it
happens, she'll probably have a good old laugh
about it.'

No, I didn't find it terribly convincing either.
Beth was going to go ballistic.

Tony went to the library to wait for his lift,
Jan and I walked across the campus towards
Main Gate.

Jan said, 'It'll be great if you, me and Tony
get parts, won't it?'

I said, 'Beth's going to have a problem with
it.'

Jan made a biologically feasible but uncomfortable suggestion about what Beth could do with her problem.

We were at the bike sheds. Hallo was there, struggling to mount his battered push-bike. He sort of waved; I sort of waved back.

Jan said, 'Beth doesn't own the guy!'

Hallo's voice sounded behind us. He said:

'But soft! What light through yonder window breaks?

It is the east, and Juliet is the sun.'

I turned my head, and Hallo was looking at me. He smiled, and:

Pru was seated alone at the seafront café, an untouched cup of coffee in front of her on the table. Her eyes were distant as she let her mind drift off into the record that was playing on the jukebox.

> *You and I together,*
> *Perfectly, for ever,*
> *Nothing else whatever*
> *Matters to our hearts.*

Pru was thinking of the storm, how she'd slipped on the rocks, and the warmth of Tom's arms when he had caught her. They had walked back to the road together, talking, and it had felt close. Pru knew it wasn't right to think about Tom that way when he was going out with Shaylene, but she couldn't help herself. He had lost a brother, she had lost her parents, and somehow it made a bond between them, that people who had never lost anyone close wouldn't understand. If only—

Pru's thoughts were interrupted by someone standing next to her table. She glanced up and saw Ken: weedy, bespectacled, ginger-haired Ken, with the big Adam's apple that wobbled when he swallowed. They had been good mates at High School and Uni, but Pru hadn't been in touch very often since she started working at the Wongalloo Herald.

'Well, hi there, stranger!' said Ken. 'Haven't seen you for ages.'

'I keep pretty busy,' Pru said.

'That coffee looks cold. Fancy another?'

Something about the look in Ken's eyes irritated Pru. He was acting like a dog that was fawning for attention. 'Er, better not,' she said. 'I have to get back to the office. Nice bumping into you.' She stood up and walked towards the door.

Ken watched her, and said, 'Hey, maybe we could get together some time, catch up on each other.'

'Yeah, maybe,' said Pru.

A bell jingled as Pru opened the café door and stepped outside.

Tunk tinka tunk, tinka tunk, tinka tunk . . .

9

TRUST STUFF

Beth on the phone: Big Trouble in the House of Lurve.

She said, 'Why didn't you tell me Tony was going to the auditions?'

I said, 'Because I didn't know myself, until he turned up.'

'What does he want to be in the play for anyway?'

I said, 'He's a really good actor, Beth. You should have seen him!'

Beth said, 'Huh! I suppose Jan was there?'

'She told you at break that she was going to be there.'

'Bet *she* knew Tony was going! Bet she had it all planned out.'

'She was as surprised as the rest of us,' I said.

'Bet she wasn't. If I wasn't around, she'd jump at the chance to go out with Tony!'

I thought, 'Yes, Jan would be first in the queue, but there'd be about two hundred girls standing behind her, me and Nattie included.' I said, 'It wasn't like that.'

'Like what?'

'Like what you're thinking.'

'Oh, so you're a mind reader now, are you?' said Beth. 'You think I'm worried that Jan's going to pinch Tony off me, I suppose?'

I *thought* that I thought, 'She will if you carry on like this!' – only instead of thinking it, I said it. The words barged past my brain and went straight to my mouth before I could stop them.

Beth said, '*What?*' in her Wicked Witch of the West voice.

I said, 'If you're worried about Jan, get in on the play. Do Front of House, or make-up, like Nattie. That way you can keep an eye on Tony.'

'So you reckon I can't trust him, then?' said Beth. 'Is he going off me? Has he said anything to you?'

'No!'

Beth said, 'Then I don't get it. Something must be going on. Why would Tony want to be in a play instead of going out with me?'

That did it. I said, 'It's a plot, Beth. The whole school's in on it. Mr Shepherd deliberately planned the production so that Jan would have a chance to get off with Tony, and it was all my idea. Everybody at the auditions was laughing at you behind your back!'

'Huh!' said Beth. 'Now you're just being stupid.'

I said, 'No, Beth! *You're* the one who's being stupid. Wise up or lose out!'

I banged the phone down.

Mum was watching me from the doorway of the lounge. She gave me a round of applause. 'About time,' she said.

'About time what?'

'That you stopped letting Beth rule your life,' Mum said. 'Have you any idea how much time you spend running round after that girl?'

I said, 'I don't let Beth rule my life!'

'No?' said Mum. 'She moans to you at school, then rings you up and bends your ear for hours. She's selfish, spoilt, sulky, she takes out all her bad moods on you – and what do you get out of it?'

I was goldfished: standing there with my mouth opening and closing, but no words coming out. Finally, I said, 'Yeah, you're right. What *do* I get out of it?'

Mum said, 'Welcome to the real world, kiddo!'

Next morning on the way to school, I told Nattie about the phone call.

Nattie said, 'Oh-oh! Better get ready, Beth's bound to give you the cold, silent treatment!'

'No she won't,' I said. '*I'm* not talking to *her!*'

I'd never thought of it that way round before; it felt good.

Nattie went off to her form room for registration, and I was plodding over to my form, when someone fell into step beside me. It was Hallo, bouncing along like a sparrow. He said,

'Well hi there, Suzanne! I'm going to talk to you because you look like a nice person to talk to.'

'Some people wouldn't think so,' I said.

'Then they must be total morons,' said Hallo. 'Hey, I had a dream about you last night!'

I stopped walking, turned my eyes into kebab-skewers and impaled him on them. 'You did what?' I said.

'Nothing leery, honest!' said Hallo. 'It was kind of romantic and mysterious. I was in, like this ballroom with crystal chandeliers. I saw you across the dance floor, wearing a long white dress. I walked over to you, asked you to dance and then . . . and then . . .'

'Yes?'

'You turned into a tin of baked beans,' said Hallo.

I said, 'You're on something.'

'Don't need it. The world's full of crazy stuff. Like Road Works signs.'

I said, 'Road Works signs?'

'Well sure!' said Hallo. 'You're driving in your car,' he put his hands on an imaginary steering wheel and swayed from side to side, 'and you see this sign that says – *Road Works Ahead*. That's good, because if the road ahead *didn't* work, there'd be a huge, bottomless pit that you'd drive into, and go on falling for ever. A-a-r-g-h!'

I said, 'You're . . .'

'Different?' said Hallo. 'Go on, tell me I'm different!'

'You're different.'

'Ripper!' said Hallo, grinning. 'Thanks, Suzanne. You just made my day. I think I'll do you a pencil-case.'

'A what?'

'A pencil-case.' Hallo put down his sports bag, poked about inside, and brought out a pencil-case – one of those old-fashioned ones with a sliding lid. It had been painted dayglo orange, pink and purple, with gold stars and spirals, and *HALLO* in bright red on the top. 'I paint pencil-cases for people,' said Hallo. 'This one's me.'

'You're a *pencil-case*?' I said.

'The painting's me. Kind of chaotic and confused. I did one for my kid sis that had all these peas and cabbages on it, because she really hates them.'

'What are you going to put on mine?'

'Have to wait and see,' said Hallo. He put the pencil-case back in his bag and we carried on walking. 'I think you ought to get it,' he said.

'Get what?'

'Juliet. You were just the best!'

'Jan will,' I said. 'She's much prettier than I am.'

Hallo frowned, like he was puzzled. 'You reckon?' he said.

At this point, I became aware of a lot of faces

staring at me from the form-room window, and realised that I'd been seen talking to the Class Geek in public. I went red. 'Better get a move on,' I said. 'Don't want to be late.'

I walked on as fast as I could, and left Hallo behind.

English, last lesson. Timed essay on Act One of *Romeo and Juliet*. Mr Wright was stalking the room like a hungry heron. I got my head down, managed to ignore the fact that Tony was sitting next to me, and concentrated on Mr Wright's Golden Rules for Essay Writing:
1) Start by saying what you're going to say.
2) Say it.
3) Conclude by saying that you've said it.

I wondered what grade Shakespeare would have got if he'd written the essay. Did he know he was putting all that stuff in his plays, or did he just make it up as he went along?

'Five minutes,' said Mr Wright.

I read through my essay, checking for those Disney bits that happen when your pen comes to life and writes down things you didn't mean.

'Time up!' said Mr Wright. 'Please pass your papers to the ends of the tables.'

The room relaxed just as the bell rang.

Tony turned to me and said, 'That wasn't so bad, was it?'

'It was all right,' I said.

Tony said, 'Suze, you rushing straight back home?'

'No.'

Tony said, 'You couldn't spare the time to come up to the library with me, could you? Only there's something I'd like to get straight.'

I said, 'Sure! Yes! I'm not doing anything!'

'I need to talk to a friend,' said Tony.

We didn't go into the library. We waited outside, leaning on the safety-railing around the staff car park. A few Year Ten people shot us funny looks as they walked past, and I thought, 'Read all about it! Suzanne Finch seen talking to Tony Beckwith!' I said, 'Beth?'

Tony said, 'In one. She's started playing silly whatsits with me.'

'How?'

'Oh, you know,' said Tony. 'She says I have to choose between the play and her.'

'So what's it going to be?'

'I don't see why I should have to make a choice at all!' Tony said. 'Don't get me wrong, Beth is a great girl and everything, and I wouldn't want to hurt her feelings, but it's like . . .'

'Like she's trying to rule your life?' I said. (Thanks, Mum!)

Tony sighed. 'What am I going to do, Suze?' And:

Pru and Tom walked along an avenue of gum trees in Wongalloo Park. The leaves of the gum trees

68

whispered in the breeze, blending with the shouting and laughter from the kids' playground nearby.

Pru said, 'So, Shaylene giving you a hard time?'

Tom smiled. 'Is it that obvious?'

'Why else would you ring me up and ask me to meet you here?' Pru said. A forlorn hope was shining in her eyes, but Tom didn't notice.

'She keeps blowing hot and cold,' Tom said. 'One minute everything's fine, next minute I've done something to offend her. I don't know whether I'm coming or going. Has she said anything to you about me?'

'No,' said Pru, 'but you're not the first guy she's treated this way.'

Tom sighed deeply, as if Pru had confirmed something that he suspected. 'I don't know what to do,' he said. 'I'm beginning to think . . .'

'What?'

'That I'd be better off without her.'

'I'm not saying anything,' said Pru. 'That's your decision.'

Tom came out of his gloom and looked Pru in the eyes. 'I don't know what made me call you like that, but I'm glad I did,' he said.

'No worries,' said Pru. 'I don't mind listening. I'm good at it. It's part of my job.'

'And how about you? Who do you go to when you've got problems?'

'No one,' Pru said. 'I don't have any problems worth talking about.'

She turned her head away, so that Tom wouldn't

69

see the tears that had suddenly welled up in her eyes.

Tunk tinka tunk, tinka tunk, tinka tunk . . .

If Tony had asked me before, I would have been like: 'Whoo! Don't do anything to rattle Beth, because she'll give me a hard time!' Now I didn't care. I said, 'Call her bluff. Tell her you're going to do the play, and if she doesn't like it – tough!'

'Suppose she gets upset?'

'She'll get over it,' I said. I remembered the conversation at the bowling rink, and said, 'Tony, d'you like Beth, or d'you only fancy her?'

'I've been asking myself that.'

'And?'

'I don't know. Sometimes I fancy her more than I like her, other times I like her more than I fancy her, and then there are times when I don't think I do either.'

Pause; deep breath – get in there, girl!

I said, 'D'you like me?'

Tony laughed. 'Better than like, Suze,' he said. 'I trust you.'

That made it *our* conversation, something not to be shared with anyone else. Tony had given me a part of himself – his trust – and if he trusted me, it meant that he must have been thinking about me.

My insides went – WHEE!

70

10

FLAWS STUFF

I was pleased when Beth didn't ring me on Tuesday night, but I have to admit that I felt guilty, too. I kept remembering Year Seven, when my form had a big Anti-Suze campaign, and Beth had been the only person I could talk to about it. She was the one who suggested I should take exercise and start eating sensibly. She didn't do it tactfully, but then there are times when you need to be told things straight, and she made me see that my weight problem was *mine*, and that I could deal with it myself, which gave me a shot of self-confidence.

The trouble was, I'd been so grateful to Beth for being my friend when no one else wanted to be, that I'd put up with a lot more from her than I would have from anyone else, and as long as I kept taking it, Beth went on handing it out. Sure, she was selfish and spoilt, and all the things that Mum had said – but it was partly my fault. Like if I'd been a *really* good mate, I would have told her when she was being obnoxious instead of agreeing with her all the time.

I nearly rang her to warn her about what

Tony had said, but then I thought, 'No. Beth's got to learn that the world doesn't revolve around her. I'm not going to come running every time she's in trouble – not any more!'

Mates, eh? Sometimes you look at them and think, 'My God, I actually chose to be friends with you lot!'

Like a lot of stuff, mates are something you only have yourself to blame for.

The cast list went:

Romeo – Anthony Beckwith
Juliet – Janine Harker
then, a bit further down,
Mercutio – Harold Gluck
and even further down, near the bottom,
Nurse – Suzanne Finch.

Hallo said, 'Well that's cool, I get stabbed! I'm out of it in Act Three.'

I said, 'It's all right for you. I've got to play the Nurse!'

'Top part!' said Hallo.

I said, 'The Nurse is about five hundred years old, and she says, *alack the day*. How am I going to say – *alack the day* – without sounding like a complete idiot?'

'Acting,' said Hallo. 'It'll be a challenge. My part's easy, because Mercutio's a bit of a head-case, but you've got to transform yourself from a bright, attractive young woman into a frumpy old biddy.'

72

I said, 'I can do without the sarcasm, thanks very much.'

Hallo said, 'I wasn't being sarcastic.'

Jan was behind us, leaning against a radiator. Nattie was with her. Jan was in total shock; she said, 'Oh, wow! Unreal!'

Nattie said, 'And Tony's playing Romeo!'

Jan said, 'Unreal! Oh, wow!'

I said, 'You'll have to kiss him, on stage, in front of an audience.'

Jan said, 'Oh, unreal! Wow!'

'Another great acting challenge!' said Hallo. 'You'll have to convince everybody that you're madly in love with the guy.'

Jan, Nattie and I stared at him.

'What did I say?' said Hallo.

I went outside, and Hallo tagged along. I was too depressed about the Nurse thing to mind. Just to make my day, Beth was walking up towards the Drama Hall, and when she saw me she turned round and headed off in the opposite direction.

I said, 'Super!'

'Isn't that Beth Walsh?' said Hallo.

'Uh-hu.'

'I thought she was a friend of yours?'

'Not just at the moment.'

'Loads of guys in our year are crazy for her,' said Hallo. 'Can't see it myself.'

I said, 'Uh?'

'She's OK if you go for the Barbie type, but personally I prefer something a little less plastic,' said Hallo. 'Beth looks so perfect, it's boring. I like people with flaws. They're much more interesting.'

'What d'you mean, flaws?'

Hallo said, 'Well, um, like, you know – freckles, for instance.'

'You're weird,' I said.

'Not when you get to know me,' said Hallo. 'When you get to know me, you find out that I'm *totally* weird.'

I laughed. Hallo was good at making me laugh, even though I felt embarrassed about being seen with him.

Hallo said, 'Well that's better! I've cheered you up.'

I said, 'Thanks, Hallo, but I can't stand round here being cheered up all day. I have to—'

'Wait up!' said Hallo. 'I've got something for you.'

It hadn't registered that all the time we'd been talking, Hallo had been clutching a lilac paper bag, but it registered now because he held it out to me.

'What's this?' I said.

'A pressie.'

'For me?'

'Sure!'

'Why d'you want to give me a present?'

Hallo went pink. 'Because it's Wednesday,' he said. 'Wednesdays are good. They fill in the gap between Tuesday and Thursday better than any other day of the week could.' He waved the bag. 'Go on, take it! It's not doggy-do, or anything.'

Inside the bag was a pencil-case, painted bright blue, with a pattern of tiny baked-bean tins. On the lid, in lime green letters, it said – LIVE WILD OR DIE.

I said, 'This is *me?*'

Hallo said, 'Sort of. Like, everybody eats baked beans, but nobody thinks about them. They kind of take them for granted.'

'And that's me, is it? I'm the sort of person other people take for granted.'

'Ah!' said Hallo. 'But the words on the lid mean that inside you there's a wild and crazy girl waiting to break out.'

I said, 'What makes you think I'm a wild and crazy girl?'

Hallo said, 'I can dream, can't I?'

And I went:

Pru and Ken were in Pru's car, parked on the seafront, facing the ocean. A full moon had come up, shining silver on the restless waves.

Pru had started to talk about Tom, and somehow it had all slipped out without her meaning it to. Confessing her feelings to Ken had been like confessing them to herself, and she had burst into tears. She was calmer now, drying her face with the handkerchief that Ken had given to her.

Ken said, 'If you've got it that bad, why don't you tell the guy?'

75

'There'd be no point,' Pru said with a sniff. 'It's obvious he doesn't care about me as much as I care about him. He thinks of me as just . . .'

'A friend?'

'I guess.' Pru shook her head. 'I was like this all through High School and Uni, wasn't I? I'd fall for the wrong guy, and when my feelings got hurt I'd come running to you for sympathy. How come you were always there for me, Ken? I don't know why you put up with me – I don't know why you're putting up with me now.'

Ken said, 'It's no bother. Mates are for sharing the bad times as well as the good, aren't they?'

Pru smiled bravely. 'Hey,' she said, 'd'you ever think that it's a pity you and I didn't . . .?'

'Didn't what?'

'Feel anything but friendship for each other? That there's never been anything deeper between us?'

'Yeah, I know,' said Ken. 'It's a crying shame, isn't it?'

Tunk tinka tunk, tinka tunk, tinka . . .

'Suzanne?' said Hallo.

'Hmm?'

'You all right? You just went—'

'I was thinking about some people I know,' I said. 'I'm fine, really.'

Only I wasn't really fine, I was confused. I got into *Love Street* when I needed to escape from a tricky situation – so why had it hap-

pened now? I wasn't doing anything tricky –
just talking to Hallo.

I got home from school and got straight into
Science and Maths. The good thing about
doing homework is that it stops you from
thinking about yourself, and not thinking
about myself was such a relief that when the
phone rang at a quarter to five, I felt irritated
at having to answer it.

I said, 'Hello?'

'Hello, Suze? It's Tony.'

My stroppiness was replaced by a tickly,
whirly, up-up-and-away feeling. I said, 'Tony!
Hi!'

Tony said, 'Has Beth rung you?'

'No.'

'Well, she might. I told her about the play,
like you said.'

'How did she take it?'

'She finished with me.'

Tony didn't sound too heartbroken, but I
thought he might be playing Big Boys Don't
Cry, so I said, 'Don't tell me, let me guess.
You want me to go and see Beth to talk her
into giving you a second chance.'

'No,' said Tony. 'I wanted to say thanks,
actually. What you said to me yesterday really
helped. I don't think Beth and I were going
anywhere. I feel a lot better now it's all cleared
up.'

Despite myself, I felt a twinge of sympathy for Beth.

Tony said, 'Good news about the play, isn't it?'

'Great!'

'Jan's pretty excited about it, isn't she? She rang me just now.'

I said, 'Did she really?'

'Yeah, to congratulate me. That was nice of her. She said she was looking forward to acting with me.'

'I'm sure she is,' I said.

'I like Jan a lot,' said Tony. 'Makes a change for me to be friends with a girl without, you know, getting involved.'

I thought, 'You poor sucker! You've got no idea, have you?'

When Mum came home from work, I made her a cup of tea and told her about the play. She was pleased. 'The Nurse is an important role,' she said.

I said, 'Yeah, but she's strange too. She helps Romeo and Juliet get together because she wants them to be happy, but it all goes wrong and they end up dead.'

'But if they didn't, it wouldn't be a tragic love story, and nobody would ever have heard of them.'

I said, 'Why do people get such a big kick out of watching things go wrong for other people?'

'Because they're glad it's not happening to them,' said Mum.

And I thought, 'Hmm! The main characters drop like flies, but the Nurse survives. She doesn't have to die for love, she only tries to give it a helping hand. Romeo and Juliet are the screwed-up ones!'

In fact, maybe the Nurse wasn't such a bad part after all.

11

REHEARSALS STUFF

Now I can see that part of my problem was that I was expecting Romance to be wide-screen: dinners for two, with eyes shining in candle-glow; embraces on mountain tops, with the wind scattering glittering ice crystals from the branches of pine trees; Juliet's moonlit balcony. Romance was always staged, it never just happened.

I didn't know it could be small, and quiet, and as ordinary as sharing a bag of chips with someone. I also didn't know that you can be right in the middle of it and not even notice.

Ever been in a school production? You start off like – 'Hey! This could be fun!' – and then rehearsals take up more and more of your time, and more and more of your brain, until the play dominates your entire life. You even dream about it.

Unexpected friendships develop, because there are long stretches when you're hanging around waiting for your bit, so you find yourself talking to people you don't know.

Expected friendships develop too – like Tony and Jan.

Jan's technique was completely different from Beth's. Beth went in for the maximum volume, all-guns-blazing, stop-at-nothing approach. Jan was more laid-back and take-it-or-leave it, except you knew that whoever she was coming-on to wasn't going to leave it.

She started off talking to Tony about the play: 'Tony, what about if, in this scene, we . . .?' Then it was just talking – 'If we're going to play two people in love, it'd be a good idea for us to get to know each other better, wouldn't it?' From there it was shared jokes, intense whispers and lots of eye-contact.

I started talking to Hallo – or, to be strictly accurate, Hallo started talking to me. Like, every time I was on my own because Jan was occupied with Tony, I'd turn round and Hallo would be there, talking. After a while, I started talking back to him, and pretty soon I noticed how if Hallo wasn't at a rehearsal, it wasn't as good as when he was. I forget a lot of what we said, but bits stand out in my memory.

He told me about an Outback holiday he'd been on, camping on the bank of a tidal creek. He described the way the sun came up, the sounds of the birds, the changing colours of the sky reflected in the water, and it was as if I'd been there with him.

I said, 'You ought to write that down, Hallo. You're a bit of a poet on the quiet, aren't you?'

'Well for sure!' Hallo said. 'Poems just drip off my tongue. I write loads, but I never show them to anybody.'

'Why not?'

'Are you kidding?' said Hallo. 'People think I'm crazy enough as it is. If they found out I write poetry as well . . .!'

I said, 'I'd like to read some – and I wouldn't tell anybody about it if you didn't want me to.'

Hallo said, 'Well thank you, Suzanne.'

'Hallo,' I said, 'how come you never call me Suze?'

'Because I haven't been invited.'

'You're invited,' I said.

Hallo gave me a big smile that made me smile back.

Next day, he showed me one of his poems. I figured that, being Hallo, it would be curly silver writing on purple paper – but it was neatly printed in black felt-tip on a sheet of blank A4.

It went:

FRECKLES

Freckles get lots of heckles
But I think they're good –
Like a wood with falling leaves
In the breeze.
You can play Join-the-Dots
With your freckly spots
And make a picture of a baked-bean can
Or spell out a nice name,
Like Suzanne.

I said, 'It's really good!'

'Keep it,' said Hallo. 'When I'm rich and famous you can sell it to a magazine and tell them about how you were—'

'How I was what?'

'Er . . . how you used to know me when I was the Sad Loser of Cressfield Comp.'

'You're not sad,' I said. 'You're one of the funniest people I know.'

Hallo looked hard at me, and just for a second I thought he was going to tell me something really serious, but then he seemed to change his mind. He said, 'Yeah, well, you know how it is with clowns. Under the greasepaint smile there's an aching heart.'

I laughed. I thought he was joking.

And that, in case you were wondering, is how dumb you can get.

I was walking home with Jan after a rehearsal, and she was fizzing like a firework-fuse. She said, 'It's going to happen!'

'What is?'

'Tony and I is – are. I've got it all worked out.' She paused for me to say, 'Well?'

I said, 'Well?'

Jan said, 'He's coming round my house on Sunday afternoon, and we're going to try the balcony scene.'

Just for a sec, I had a flash about something to do with ropes and pulleys, then I twigged that Jan was talking about *Romeo and Juliet*. I said, 'And that's going to make it happen?'

'Tony's like really, really shy about having to kiss me in front of everybody, so I said it'd be better if we practised it on our own first.'

She made it sound easy. Just – 'Oh, hey, Tony, how about a little private kissing on Sunday afternoon?' You had to be Jan to get away with it.

Jan said, 'Seen Beth recently?'

'We're still not talking,' I said.

'Haven't you heard the latest? She's going out with Craig Muir.'

I said, '*Craig Muir?*'

Craig Muir was in Year Eleven, dishy but dense, and a notorious heart-mangler.

I thought, 'I get it! Beth's going out with Craig so that if Tony goes out with Jan, she can say she finished with him to go out with Craig, and if Tony doesn't go out with Jan, Beth can dump Craig and say that—'

I gave up on it because it was too complicated, and anyway, just then:

Tom was alone at the bar of The Blue Cockatoo. *Josie was working a late shift behind the bar, looking pretty in her uniform.*

'*Same again,*' *said Tom.*

Josie wiped a cloth along the bar. '*Don't you think you've had enough, Tom?*' *she said.* '*I don't know what your problem is, but you won't find the answer inside a beer bottle. It wouldn't have anything to do with Shaylene, would it?'*

'My, doesn't word get out fast?' said Tom. He tilted his bottle and stared moodily at the dregs in the bottom. 'Soon as I think I've found that someone special, something happens to spoil it.'

'Maybe you've been looking in the wrong place,' said Josie.

Tom smiled wryly. 'Tell me about it!' he said.

Josie said, 'Look, Tom, I know this is none of my business, so you can tell me to rack off if you want, but I don't think you and Shaylene were ever right for each other. She's too cold, too manipulative.'

'That so?' said Tom. 'Who is right for me, then?'

'Someone you can have fun with, someone who won't cause you any hassles.'

'Sounds good,' said Tom. 'Just one problem – there's no one like that around.'

'Isn't there?' said Josie. 'Maybe you should look closer, Tom.'

Tom stared at Josie. 'What, you mean – you?' he said.

Josie said, 'You ought to give me a try. Call me, any time. You know the number, don't you?'
Tunk tinka tunk, tinka tunk, tinka . . .

Jan said, 'Beth's really scraping the bottom of the barrel, isn't she? She's playing with fire.'

I said, 'D'you get fires at the bottoms of barrels?'

Jan frowned. 'You spend too much time

talking to Hallo,' she said. 'It's warping your brain.'

And I wasn't the only one with a warped brain, not according to the goss anyway. A week or so after Beth started going out with Craig, I started hearing some pretty ugly things around school. Craig was supposed to have sounded off to his mates about how hot and how easy Beth was, and that she'd gone all the way on the third date, and that it was a new record for him.

First time I heard about it, I thought, 'Nah! Beth's not that stupid.'

But then I started to wonder. She must have been really peed off about Tony, maybe so peed off that she'd got in over her head. Craig was notorious for being the kind of guy who only went out with girls for one thing, and after Tony, Beth would have been desperate to hang onto him, for *I'm the girl who can handle Craig Muir* points.

'Get outta here!' I told myself. 'Hell hath no fury like a woman scorned and stuff, but Beth wouldn't be that dumb . . . would she?'

I had a bad feeling about it, and kind of wished I could talk to Beth and find out what was really going on, but I didn't have time because . . .

First rehearsal without scripts – lots of people smacking their foreheads and saying words that

Mr Shepherd pretended not to hear. All he said was, 'Again, from the top!'

It was the scene where the Nurse goes looking for Romeo, and finds his mates. Mercutio makes fun of her with some rude puns, and Hallo delivered them so there was no doubt about what they meant. The scene gradually came together: Hallo and I got to know each other's timing well enough to leave just the right gap before saying a line, and Hallo started imitating my movements behind my back, just like a cheeky teenager would.

At the end, Mr Shepherd took us both aside. 'Tone it down a bit,' he said.

'Weren't we any good?' said Hallo.

Mr Shepherd said, 'You're too good. At the moment, this is The Nurse and Mercutio Show, not *Romeo and Juliet*. Try being more shocked at what Mercutio says, Suzanne.'

'I thought the Nurse was enjoying herself,' I said. 'Mercutio's flirting with her, like he can see through her respectability, and it makes her feel young again. She pretends to be angry with him, but really she's flattered.'

'Suze,' said Mr Shepherd, 'this is a school production. You say the lines in the right order, and get off without tripping over the scenery. Save the rest for the West End.'

Miffed is the word for what I was. As Mr Shepherd walked off to have a word with Tony, I said, 'This is impossible! He wants us to be good, but he doesn't want us to be good. How are we supposed to do that?'

Hallo said, 'Have you ever been in love, Suze?'

I was so surprised, I didn't think. I said, 'Only all the time.'

'Oh, yeah!' said Hallo. He nodded towards Tony. 'Mr Soulful Eyes, right?'

'How did you know?'

'Because I'm an incredibly sensitive, caring person with an almost paranormal ability to intuit other people's feelings,' Hallo said.

I said, 'How about you? Have you ever been in love?'

'Once – I think,' said Hallo. 'There was this girl back in Oz, Emily. She lived on our street. I used to watch from the front room window when she walked past the house. She had this great walk, you know? Sort of flowing. And when the sun shone through her hair, it was like a halo glowing round her head. I started to wait for her at the front garden gate, hoping she'd notice me and say hello or something. Best thing about her was, she had this snaggle tooth that sort of—'

I said, 'Hallo, why are you telling me this?'

'I thought it'd stop you worrying about what Mr Shep said. Did it work?'

'Yes,' I said. 'What happened? Did Emily talk to you?'

'Nah!' said Hallo. 'I wrote her this really

great poem about how I felt, but I decided not to give it to her.'

'Why not?'

Hallo said, 'It was better to keep her at a distance, so she could stay perfect. If I'd given her the poem, she might have gone YEUK! and that would've spoilt my dream. Besides, I was eight years old and she was twenty-two.'

12

GREYS STUFF

On Sunday I woke up with a bad attack of the greys. The greys is my name for the blues, because when you've got the blues, nothing is blue, is it? More sort of colourless and miserable. Up until Year Eight, the greys had been easy for me to deal with – a couple of packets of crisps, a Mars bar and a chocolate milkshake generally did the trick – but I'd sworn off comfort-eating, so I went for a walk around the lakes.

The lakes sounds glamorous, doesn't it? Like, snowcapped Toblerone-type mountains with expanses of silvery water at their feet, and maybe some yachts gliding past like swans.

No chance! The lakes are basically three holes in the ground, left over from a gravel-quarrying business. They're full of water, but there's no fish in them, or ducks, just green slimy stuff that coagulates into lumps. There are signs up saying, 'It is prohibited to swim in the gravel pits', and I've always wondered why, because who'd want to? I mean, what sort of person looks at a pond full of goo and thinks,

'I'm going to rip off my kit and go skinny dipping!'?

The lakes are ugly, repellent and depressing: a perfect place to take the greys.

The sky was overcast and a damp, cold wind was blowing. The fallen leaves had gone down to a mush that oozed dark-brown liquid when I stepped on it.

I did Tony first – Impossible Tony, who was probably getting it together with Jan at that precise moment. Tony treated me as a friend, but that wasn't enough; it didn't help the ache that I was carrying around. What would it be like to hold him, and have him to myself, and know that I was more important to him than anyone else? What was wrong with me, anyway? I was fourteen and I didn't have a boyfriend, so something had to be wrong somewhere. Maybe it was never going to get better, and I'd spend my whole life on my own.

I tortured myself with that stuff for a while, and then I went on to Beth. I was worried about her: she was going to get hurt, and she might land herself in real trouble, because Craig Muir hung out with a wild crowd. She needed a good talking-to, and I was the best person to do it, but she wasn't in any mood to listen to me.

And the play was three weeks away from opening – close enough to be worrying.

And I was getting behind with coursework because of rehearsals. Teachers had extended my deadlines, but I still had to get the work done.

The lakes didn't help me get rid of the greys, but at least I knew what was causing them – life. I had to do something positive, so I went home and started a History essay. School work was the only bit of the greys I could control.

Two phone calls interrupted me. The first one was from Jan.

I said, 'How did it go this afternoon?'

Jan said, 'Phwoar!'

'All right, then?'

Jan said, 'I was – he was – it was – he's a brilliant snogger! He . . .'

She went into a description that made me consider becoming a vegetarian.

'You're going out with him, then?' I said.

'Not exactly. He hasn't asked me yet, but I'm sure he's going to. You don't snog like he does without meaning it.'

'So are you and Tony an item, or what?'

'I'm working on it,' said Jan.

The second phone call came half an hour later: Tony.

He said, 'Suze, what does Jan think about me?'

'A lot,' I said.

'Oh.'

'Why, oh?'

Tony said, 'I was afraid of that. I think she might have got the wrong impression. See, we got together this afternoon to do a scene from the play, and we had to kiss and . . . well, I got a bit carried away.'

'Don't worry,' I said. 'I'm sure Jan wasn't offended.'

'She didn't seem to be. Actually, she was quite . . .'

'Keen?' I said.

'Enthusiastic,' said Tony. 'She doesn't want to go out with me or anything, does she?'

'Put it this way, if you asked her, she'd say yes.'

Tony said, 'Oh, dear!'

Funny reaction – not what I was used to hearing from boys who found out that Jan wanted to go out with them.

I said, 'What's the matter? Don't you like Jan?'

'Course I do!' said Tony. 'Only . . .'

'Yes?'

'Juliet.'

'Pardon?'

'Juliet,' said Tony. 'I don't know if what happened was me kissing Jan, or Romeo kissing Juliet. It all got sort of mixed-up together.'

'You mean, where did acting end and real life begin?'

'Right!' said Tony. 'D'you have to be in love to act being in love, or can you be a little bit in love and then pretend that you're *really* in love?'

I said, 'How can you be a little bit in love? Like only up to your toe nails?'

There was a pause, then Tony said, 'Have you been talking to Hallo?'

'Yes. Why?'

'You just sounded like him.'

'Is that a compliment or an insult?'

'Pass,' said Tony. 'What d'you think I should do, Suze?'

I wanted to say, 'Forget about Jan! Come round here and snog me, you great steaming hunk!' I said, 'Ask Jan out. If you go out with her, you'll be able to work out whether it's her or Juliet that you're interested in.'

Tony said, 'But supposing I do, and then it turns out that I don't like Jan as much as she wants me to? If she's angry with me, it'll make things awkward for the play, won't it?'

'It's going to be more awkward if you don't ask her out,' I said. 'She'll think you were stringing her along.'

'But if I do, she might get the idea that I want it to be more than it is.'

'And what is it?'

'I don't know,' said Tony. 'I'm confused!'

So was I. The worst part of being someone that other people tell their troubles to, is that other people ring up and tell you their troubles, and they get to be your troubles as well.

I listened to Tony for ten more minutes, then told him to let things carry on as they were, and see if they sorted themselves out.

I put down the phone, and –

At first, Pru wasn't sure that it was Shaylene who was hunched over a table in the darkest corner of The Blue Cockatoo, *but then Shaylene raised her head to drain a glass of wine, and Pru saw her face.*

Pru approached the table cautiously and said, 'Shaylene?'

Shaylene looked terrible. She wasn't wearing make-up, her face was pale and drawn, and her usually glossily groomed hair was as dry and unkempt as a pile of hay. Pru had never seen Shaylene dead-drunk before, and it came as a shock.

'Well look who it isn't,' Shaylene said, slurring her words. 'Little Miss Butter-Wouldn't-Melt. I bet you knew all along, didn't you?'

'Knew what?' said Pru.

'About him and her.'

'Excuse me?' said Pru, frowning deeply. 'I have no idea what you're talking about, Shaylene.'

'Tom and Josie,' said Shaylene. 'I had a sick headache this afternoon, so I left work early. I went home, and there they were, together on the sofa. How long have they been carrying on behind my back?'

Pru was totally bewildered. 'Tom and Josie?' she gasped.

'It doesn't matter,' said Shaylene. 'She's welcome to him. He's nothing but a two-timing rat. If I never see him again, it'll be too soon as far as I'm concerned.'

As if to mock her words, the door of the pub

swung back, and Tom and Josie entered. Josie was holding Tom's arm and leaning into him.

Pru stared at them in disbelief, and tears began to roll down her face. She ran out of The Blue Cockatoo *ignoring Tom's, 'Hi!' as she rushed past.*

Tom said, 'What's wrong with Pru? Should I go after her?'

'I think you should leave her alone,' said Josie. 'She can't handle seeing us together. That's why she left in such a hurry.'

'But why should Pru be upset about us?'

Josie's eyebrows went up in surprise. 'You mean you don't know?' she said. 'You really *don't know?'*

Tunk tinka tunk, tinka . . .

I thought, 'Help! I need someone to talk to! I need sympathy! I need cheering up!'

So I got out the telephone directory, and looked up Hallo's number.

'Yeah?' A man's voice, gravelly Australian accent.

I said, 'Mm, oh, hello. Is Harold there please?'

'You wanna talk to 'im?'

Like, why else would I be on the phone?

I said, 'I would, actually, if it's convenient.'

'I'll get 'im,' the man said, then bellowed, 'Harry? Blower!'

In the background, I could hear a food-processor rattling, a telly blaring, the thumping of techno music; then a door slammed, there was a sound like a skip being emptied down a flight of stairs, and Hallo said, 'You're talking to him.'

I said, 'Ha—'

'What's the matter, Suze?' said Hallo. 'You sound upset.'

I said, 'I haven't said anything yet.'

'Didn't have to,' said Hallo. 'I'm Dr Intuition, remember? What is it?'

I said, 'I'm not upset upset. Not really. Not much. You see . . .'

And I told him about me, Beth, Jan, Nattie, *Romeo and Juliet*, coursework, the greys – everything.

When I'd finished, Hallo said, 'Well I think Tony Beckwith doesn't know when he's well off.'

I said, 'Yeah, but—'

Hallo said, 'No buts. The guy's a waste of space. He doesn't need a shoulder to cry on, he needs a boot up the backside!'

I said, 'He's only trying—'

'Trying, nothing!' said Hallo. 'He's got all these amazing girls doing somersaults for him, and all he can do is whinge about it! He must enjoy being miserable – it's the only explanation! I dream about having problems like his!'

I said, 'He's—'

Hallo said, 'Take a deep breath.'

I took a deep breath.

Hallo said, 'Repeat after me – Tony Beckwith . . .'

'Tony Beckwith . . .'

' . . . is a total jerk.'

' . . . is a total jerk,' I said. Then I laughed, because Hallo was right. Tony *was* a jerk – nice, good-looking, but still a jerk.

And I was cured – whap! Just like that. Tony was still fanciable and everything, but I wasn't in love with him, and maybe I never had been. He was gorgeous, sensitive and knew all the right things to say, but when it came to walking the talk he was useless.

It wasn't Tony's fault; he couldn't help it. He was like one of those puppies that's so cute, everybody has to pick it up and cuddle it, until in the end it doesn't know who's who or where it belongs; or one of those kids who causes a queue at the newsagent's when he can't make up his mind what sweets he wants to buy. *Spoilt for choice* – as the cliché goes.

Year Ten was this huge Relationships Machine, churning out couples in every possible combination, and because Tony was new, the machine had gone haywire. He hadn't set out for loads of girls to fall in love with him, and he didn't know what to do about it when they did.

13

DRESS-REHEARSAL STUFF

Craig finished with Beth. I heard the goss, and I saw her walking round school, looking pale and upset but giving off Don't-Talk-To-Me-Vibes. She was still being stubborn, and so was I. I thought, 'This time she's going to have to come to me!'

Tony did ask Jan out, but it wasn't what she'd been expecting. She told me about it in the Sandwich Room one lunchtime. She said, 'I can't work out what he wants. I don't know if *he* knows what he wants. After that Sunday I thought . . . you know . . . but all he did was talk! He didn't even kiss me goodnight.'

'Talking's nice,' I said.

'Yeah, but he talked about his old girlfriends, and how they'd given him a bad time. It was like they were on his mind more than I was.'

I said, 'Maybe he wanted you to get to know him.'

'I do want to get to know him,' said Jan, 'but I don't want to know all his exes as well! They might as well have been there, staring at us! And then, he started going on about you!'

'Me?' I said. 'What did he say?'

'Oh, you're wonderful, you are! You're understanding, and easy to talk to. He thinks the sun shines out of your butt.'

'So-rry!'

'Not a problem,' said Jan. 'I just wish he'd said it about me! Then after you, it was the play – on and on and on. D'you know what he asked me? *If Romeo and Juliet were alive today, d'you think they'd go to MacDonalds?* I was like – UH?'

'Do they have a MacDonald's in Verona?' I said.

Jan said, 'If they do, they probably have Romeo and Juliet burgers – loads of ketchup, and served with daggers stuck through them!'

The play really got into gear. The sets were built, the lights were put into place and the costumes arrived. The boys were embarrassed about having to wear ballet tights, and cracked lots of jokes about frozen cod-pieces. (Ho, ho, ho!)

Tony wore a black velvet doublet with slashes in the sleeves to show off the red satin lining – and he looked scrummy in it. Jan had a long white gown with floaty sleeves – knockout, natch. Hallo's doublet was canary yellow, which clashed with his hair so much that people were going, 'Excuse me, would you mind turning down the volume on your head?' My costume was large and brown, with a white cap and apron. It made me look like a cross between a cottage loaf and Mrs Tiggiwinkle.

There were costume calls, make-up calls, photo calls, sword-fighting lessons (for the boys), Act run-throughs, full run-throughs and technicals. We were jabbed with safety-pins, smothered in Leichener and blinded by stage lights. Mr Shepherd's temper got shorter as the bags under his eyes got bigger and darker. Rehearsals took up most evenings, and the entire Sunday before the opening night on Tuesday: complete run-through in the morning, a break for lunch, and then a full dress-rehearsal.

Like most people, I brought a packed lunch, but I was too excited to eat much of it. The cast was keyed-up, the tension was like being in a balloon that's about to go pop, and the noise in the Green Room was life-threatening. Other people's jitters made me jittery, and I wished Hallo was there for me to talk to, but he'd ridden his bike home for lunch. Eventually I couldn't take it any more, so I went outside to try to relax. The contrast was amazing – just another boring Sunday. I let the quiet nothing of it creep into me.

Tony came out through the Drama Hall door and joined me. 'It's like a madhouse in there, isn't it?'

I said, 'Anyone started climbing the walls yet?'

Tony smiled, then his eyes went: BOY WITH PROBLEM.

'How are things with you and Jan?' I said.

'Don't ask!' said Tony. 'I've been trying to get her to ease up and take things slowly, but that's not Jan's way, is it?'

'No. Jan's more like a traction engine – she's slow to start, but once she gets going nothing can stop her!'

'I don't know, Suze!' Tony said. 'It's all a mess. It was a mistake for Jan and I to get involved in the first place. I thought I was going to fall for her in a big way, but then it sort of fizzled out.'

'So you're in love with Juliet?' I said.

'I'm starting to think so. Juliet's fiery, and impulsive, and passionate!' Just for a second, his face lit up and he was so beautiful that it made the ache come back – then the light went out.

'Sounds like Jan,' I said.

'Jan's a bit like Juliet,' said Tony, 'but not enough to . . .' He laughed and shook his head. 'I'm in love with a character from one of Shakespeare's plays,' he said. 'I must be going mental!'

I said, 'No, you've just had a flash of what the Great Love of your Life is going to be like – only when you meet her, don't drink the poison.'

Tony said, 'I've got to tell Jan the truth, haven't I?'

'Yes.'

Tony looked away, and said, 'Would you talk to her for me? You're much better at explaining things than I am.'

And:

The doorbell rang. Pru went to answer it, and found Tom standing in the porch. 'Can we talk?' he said hesitantly.

'If you like,' said Pru. 'You'd better come in.'

They went into the lounge. Tom seemed awkward. He ran his hand through his hair and said, 'Why didn't you tell me how you felt, Pru? I had no idea that—'

'It would have made some sort of difference?' said Pru. 'You were too wrapped-up with Shaylene – or was it Josie?'

Tom looked as if he were going to get angry, but his anger suddenly left him. 'I guess I've made a real mess of things, haven't I?' he said. 'I only went out with Shaylene and Josie because I thought you weren't interested. If I'd known, things would've been a lot different.'

'Don't give me that, Tom!' Pru snapped. 'You've been playing with us all, haven't you? You had the three of us dancing on a string, and that's just the way you wanted it. You're so up yourself, you couldn't care less who gets hurt.'

Tom hung his head. 'I deserved that,' he said. 'But you're wrong about one thing. I care that you've been hurt. That's the last thing I wanted to

103

do. I came here to say that I'm sorry, and to ask you if—'

Pru held out her hand to stop him. 'Before you say anything else, I think there's something you should know,' she said.

'Oh?'

Pru said, 'I'm leaving Love Street for good. I made up my mind last night. I phoned my aunt and uncle in Queensland, and they told me I can stay with them until I get a place of my own. My uncle's sure I'll be able to get a job with one of the papers up there.'

'You're not doing this because of me, are you?' said Tom.

Pru laughed. 'Don't kid yourself,' she said 'Love Street is where I lived with my parents. I stayed here because I wanted to feel close to their memories. But now I've done some growing up, I understand that memories don't belong to a place, they're something you carry inside you wherever you are. It's time for me to move on.

Tunk tinka tunk, tinka tunk, tinka . . .

I said, 'Sorry, Tony. I'm not going to let you lay that one on me. It wouldn't be fair to me, or to Jan.'

'I know!' said Tony. 'It's just . . . I hate hurting people's feelings.'

I said, 'Sometimes you have to, and it's better to do it sooner than later.'

'You're right,' said Tony. He looked at me as

104

if it was the first time we'd met. 'How did you get to know so much about people, Suze?'

I said, 'From this really good soap opera I watch.'

'Which one?'

'You wouldn't have heard of it,' I said.

There were a few hitches at the dress-rehearsal. The lighting box didn't quite have its act together, Hallo missed an entrance because his sword got caught in the scenery, and half the Capulet tomb fell down – but otherwise it was fine, and when Mr Shepherd talked to us about it, he seemed pleased. 'All right, people!' he said. 'I want you all to go home and forget about the play until Tuesday. First make-up call is at six, and don't be late.'

I got changed, scrubbed off my make-up, and left. Outside, I saw Hallo in the middle of the empty car park. He was holding his bike, and staring up at the sky.

I walked over to him and said, 'What are you doing?'

He said, 'See that big star up there? I'm trying to work out whether it's a star or a planet.'

'How d'you tell the difference?'

'Well, stars sort of wibble, but planets shine with a steady light,' said Hallo. 'So is that wibbling, or steady, or what?'

I looked, but I couldn't tell because I had face cream in my eyes, which made everything wibble. Then I saw the star move. I said, 'Hallo, it's an aeroplane.'

'And I'm a dork!' said Hallo. 'What d'you reckon to Ye Olde Production, Suze? Hollywood, here we come?'

'Definitely!'

'I think we should stick a bit of techno in to add to the teen appeal!' Hallo began to twitch like a robot with a short-circuit, and put on a weird, mechanical voice. 'R-R-R-Romeo, Romeo! Wherefore art thou R-R-R-Romeo!'

'Perhaps not,' I said.

Hallo switched back to himself. 'I expect you've got to go straight back home now,' he said.

'Too right! Big date tonight.'

'Really?'

'With my French books. I've got a test tomorrow.'

'Oh,' said Hallo. 'No chance of tempting you into a coffee at my place then?'

'Sorry.'

'Coke? Pepsi? Bucket of cocoa?'

'Maybe some other time,' I said.

'OK, no worries. I'll look forward to it.'

'Bye!' I said.

'Bye!' said Hallo.

I was nearly at the Main Gate, when I heard the ticking of bike wheels, and Hallo overtook me, and rode the bike in a circle, with me at the centre. 'Wait up, Suze,' he said. 'I want to ask you something.'

'What?'

'I was wondering if you might . . . I mean, if you'd ever consider . . . if you'd like to . . .?'

'What?'

'Er . . . be in another play, some time.'

'I haven't got this one over with yet!' I said.

'Right!' said Hallo. 'Stupid question! Sorry I bothered you!' He pedalled off in the direction of his house, at great speed.

I thought, 'What's going on with him?'

Then I stopped worrying about it – it was just Hallo, being Hallo.

14

PERFORMANCE STUFF

On opening night, did I have butterflies? I had pterodactyls!

Nattie was making me up, and I was thinking, 'I need a pee. I'm going to throw up. I want to be somewhere else. Why did I volunteer to suffer like this? I must be some sort of masochist!'

I knew I wasn't the only one feeling like that, because the atmosphere in the Green Room was like a house in a horror movie, just before the Mad Slasher bursts in. People were sitting around, muttering speeches to themselves, or joking about things that might go wrong, and having hysterics.

'Nervous?' said Nattie.

'Terrified,' I said.

'You'll be fine,' said Nattie. 'Stop worrying, it's going to be great.'

Jan floated past. Her eyes looked like marbles. She said, 'What's my first line? I've forgotten my first line!'

'*How now, who calls?*' I said.

'Yes!' said Jan. 'Of course! How could I possibly forget that? Er . . . what was it again?'

Nattie finished me off, and I went to sit on my own and do Zen breathing. I covered one nostril, breathed in through the other, and let the breath out through my mouth.

Hallo came and sat next to me. 'Well, this is it, Suze,' he said.

'Y-e-e-s-s-s!' I said in a long breath.

'You hyperventilating or something?'

'No, I'm practising a meditation technique. It's supposed to calm you down by altering the carbon dioxide level in your blood.'

'Any good?'

'Not really.'

'I made this for you,' said Hallo, and he gave me a card.

On the front was a drawing of a leg in plaster and, underneath, it said: *Break a leg, Nursie darling!!!* Inside, was a poem.

> *If you need help when you're confused,*
> *Suze*
> *Is the person to choose.*
> *When you can't tell a planet from a plane,*
> *She'll explain.*
> *Suze*
> *Is good news.*

I said, 'Thanks, Hallo.'

'You're welcome,' Hallo said. He looked round the Green Room. 'You know, this is really weird. Like, we're here to put on a play

109

written by a bloke who's been dead for nearly four hundred years.'

'Must have been stage fright that killed him,' I said.

Hallo said, 'William Shakespeare! One of the greatest biros of all time. The folks dragged me and my sis round Stratford-Upon-Avon last summer. Can't have been easy for Shakespeare to write plays with all those tourists peeking in at the windows. No wonder the poor guy lost his hair . . .' and he went off into a routine about Shakespeare that made me laugh, and forget about my nerves.

Mr Shepherd gathered the cast and crew on stage and said, 'In five minutes we'll let the audience in, then it's fifteen minutes to curtain up. Believe it or not, all four nights have sold out.' There was a panicky buzz; Mr Shepherd raised his voice to cut through it. 'We've all worked hard, and we've learned that in a production, everybody depends on everybody else. The back-stage crew are just as important as the actors. Now we're here for the audience. Theatre is about illusion, and illusion is easy to destroy – so keep the noise in the Green Room down, and no peeking through the curtains to wave to your friends and family. OK, people!' Mr Shepherd smacked his right fist into his left palm, and then his nerves showed, because he got 'off the ground' mixed-up with 'on the road' and said, 'Let's get this show on the groad!'

★

Funny thing, acting. There you are, waiting to go on, a hopeless gibbering wreck with a totally blank mind, and as soon as you step into the lights, the words come by themselves. You can't really see the audience, but you feel their attention – like this big magnet that pulls the performance out of you. You say a line, and they laugh, and it's magic, and *you* did it. Two hundred-odd people reacted to something you said, and now you know why performers do what they do: not for the money, or to be famous; they're addicted to the magic.

The first night was a little shaky and slow, but we got through it without making plonkers of ourselves. The second night was better because we had a great audience – Mr Shepherd said people were moved to tears at the end. The third night was OK, but a bit flat – everybody was tired – and the last night . . . well . . . I was sad. I thought, 'What am I going to do with myself when the play's over? How am I going to fill up all that time? How will I cope when I'm not part of something?'

Hallo was sad, too. While we were waiting for curtain up, he said, 'I'm going to miss this.'

'So am I,' I said.

'Not just the acting, either. I'm going to miss the people. Like, when will I ever get the chance to talk to you again?'

I said, 'We're in the same registration group, Hallo. You can talk to me any time.'

'What, with everybody going – *Ooh look!*

111

Suze is talking to Hallo!? I don't think so. It won't be the same.'

'No, it won't.'

'I'll go back to being Wacko Hallo, and you'll go back to being Suzanne the Unattainable.'

'Unattainable?' I said.

'Well, sure!' said Hallo. 'If life was an ice-cream parlour, you'd be a sundae with whipped cream and a cherry on top, and I'd be an ice-pop.'

'You'd be a banana split,' I said.

Hallo said, 'Yeah, but without the split – just bananas! You going to the post-production bash?'

'You bet!'

'Can I grab you for a dance? I want to check-out my moves.'

'If you like,' I said.

'Can you waltz?' said Hallo.

'Yes.'

'I can't. You can teach me!'

When I wasn't on stage, I tucked myself out of the way in the wings, and watched, and it was brilliant. The fights were frightening, the love scenes were tender, the funny bits got laughs. When Mercutio/Hallo died from his stab wound, I heard someone in the audience go, 'Oh no!' But the best part was at the end, in the Capulet tomb. Tony really cried – you could see the tears shining blue in the stage lights – and I knew why he was crying. He was saying goodbye to Juliet, and he didn't know if he'd ever find her again.

Wild applause, five curtain-calls, then a big let-down. The Chairman of the School Governors stood up and made a speech about Culture and Standards and Blah, and the magic disappeared like the last spark of the last rocket on Bonfire Night.

More speeches in the Green Room, but good ones. Mr Shepherd took the mick out of everybody, then Hallo took the mick out of Mr Shepherd, and gave him the present we'd all chipped-in to buy.

Meanwhile, Tony and Jan were having a face-to-face whisper in a corner, and Jan didn't look like a Happy Bunny.

Mr Shepherd said, 'In the words of the Immortal Bard – let's party!' and everybody cheered, and one of the Front of House girls tapped me on the shoulder and said, 'Someone wants to see you outside.'

I knew it couldn't be Mum, because she'd been to Opening Night. I thought, 'Hey! A fan wants to ask me for my autograph. Cool!' But when I got out into the corridor, there was Beth.

And you know what? She looked just like the Beth I'd known in Junior School, all lost eyes.

I said, 'Beth?'

Beth didn't say anything. I thought she was getting ready to swallow her pride, then I saw that she was holding back tears.

I said, 'What's up?'
Beth said, 'I'm scared, Suze.'
'Why?'
Beth said, 'I think I'm pregnant.'
I went:

Nothing. *Love Street* wasn't there. What Beth had said was too real to be turned into a fantasy Soap Opera. There was no escape from reality this time.

Next thing I knew, Beth and I were hugging each other, and we were both crying.

15

GROWN-UP STUFF

So I missed the post-production party. Beth and I went for a long walk, and she opened up to me about Craig and how awful everything had been.

I said, 'How late are you?'

'A week.'

'Does Craig know?'

'No, and he wouldn't care if he did. He'd probably brag about it to his mates.'

'Have you told your parents?'

'I can't!' Beth groaned.

I could see the problem. How could Beth bring herself to tell her mum and dad that their Little Princess was normal, gullible, and had indulged in underage sex?

Beth said, 'My dad would kill Craig – and me. I can't face it, Suze. I took all the money out of my bank account this afternoon. I'm going to run away to London and disappear.'

She was gabbling like poultry.

I said, 'Calm down, Beth. Where are you going to stay in London? What are you going to do when your money runs out? You want to end up standing at a kerb in King's Cross?'

Some of it got through; Beth said, 'No.'

I said, 'And what about the baby? Are you going to keep it?'

'I don't know. I don't know what I'm going to do. What am I going to do, Suze?'

Good question. I don't know how many RE and Social Education lessons I'd spent discussing the ins and outs of abortion – a woman's right to decide what happens to her own body vs the rights of an unborn child – and I thought I'd made my mind up. Now that it had come down to an actual case, I wasn't so sure any more.

I said, 'The first thing you're going to do is stop panicking. Are you sure you're pregnant? Have you been to see a doctor?'

'No. I couldn't go to our doctor. She'd be bound to tell Mum and Dad.'

'Right. So get yourself a pregnancy-test kit and use it. If it's positive, you'll have to tell your parents, because you're going to need them.'

'They'll chuck me out!'

'No they won't,' I said. 'They'll go stratospheric for a while, then they'll support you. They're grown-ups, aren't they?'

Much to my surprise, I was sounding quite grown-up myself.

In her tiniest voice, Beth said, 'I can't face it on my own, Suze. I just can't. Would you . . .?'

I think I would have given anything in the world to be able to say, 'No! This is your mess, you got yourself into it, now sort it out.'

But I couldn't: this was life; I wasn't in control of the script.

You figure it's going to be easy. You'll take a bus to a part of town where no one knows you, find a chemist that opens on Sunday, breeze up to the counter and say, 'I'd like a box of sticking plasters and a packet of sugarless chewing-gum – oh, and a pregnancy-test kit, please.'

Sounds simple, doesn't it?

Watch my mouth move: it ain't.

Beth and I stuck on loads of slap to make ourselves look older, caught the bus, found the chemist's shop, then stood outside for ten minutes, working up the bottle to go in. Eventually we did, blushing like traffic-lights on stop. We got the kit, scrubbed off our make-up and went back to my place.

It was like a suspense movie.

No it wasn't! It was horrible. If the test went one way, it was going to be all right; if it went the other, Beth was looking at shame, an almighty row with her parents, and then either an abortion or having the baby – which meant carrying her pregnancy round school, people talking behind her back, all the teachers knowing. Not to mention taking care of a baby before she'd learnt how to take care of herself. What kind of life was she going to have? I imagined her living in a poky little flat, with the baby squawking in the background, not able to go out anywhere. What guy was going to be interested in her after she'd had someone else's child?

It was all the stuff they don't put in soppy magazines and TV shows; it was about romantic daydreams turning into real nightmares.

But fear is a weird thing. Beth sneaked into the upstairs loo with the kit shoved up her jumper, and two minutes later she came out crying and smiling because she'd started.

I said, 'You what?'

Beth said, 'I must have miscalculated or something. I've always been a bit irregular. Isn't it great?'

Is there a word for the feeling you get when you're relieved, annoyed, pleased, exasperated and suspect that you've been suckered into making a big hoo-ha about nothing?

I said, 'You stupid cow! Don't you dare put me through that again, ever!'

'I don't want to put myself through it again,' said Beth. 'You're right, I have been a stupid cow, but I'm never going to be stupid again.'

I said, 'I'll get you a pen. I want that in writing.'

So, a nice happy ending after all, huh? Beth and I rediscovered our friendship, and found out that life wasn't a Soap Opera after all, and that there were bits of the boy-girl thing that we weren't as ready for as we thought.

A pair of sadder but wiser teenagers, facing the future with bright smiles.

But that's not all, because . . .

Two days before the end of term, at the end of last lesson (English), Tony said, 'Suze, can I have a word?'

I said, 'Sure!' I knew Beth would be waiting, so I told Nattie to tell her that I'd ring later, and Tony and I took a slow stroll up towards the library.

Tony said, 'D'you think Beth and Jan would be friends with me, so we could all hang out together, like that time we went bowling?'

I said, 'Maybe eventually, but not now. They're still hurting.'

This was understatement of the year, because whenever Tony's name was mentioned, Beth made 'So what?' eyes, and Jan mimed poking her fingers down her throat, so they definitely weren't ready for forgive-and-forget.

'But they might be friends with me some time?' said Tony.

I said, 'Yeah.' I thought, 'Like in about ten years.'

Tony said, 'I've realised a lot since the play. I've grown up a bit, I think. See, all the time I was waiting for my Dream Girl to come along, and that was daft, because girls aren't dreams, they're real people!'

I thought, 'Well thanks for noticing!'

'And real people aren't perfect,' said Tony. 'I was expecting the girls I went out with to be perfect, and I was disappointed when they turned out to be real.'

I said, 'You sound like you've decided something.'

'I have,' said Tony. 'I've suddenly realised that the right girl for me has been staring me in the face since the first day I got here. It's you, Suze. We're the ones who ought to be going out together.'

I said, 'No.'

Tony said, 'But—!'

I said, 'You're not ready for a relationship, Tony. You take things too seriously. You're looking for Juliet, and I'm not her. We're friends, and if we go out together we'll lose that friendship. We'd spoil something really good, and I don't want to do that. Let's be happy with what we've got.'

And I walked off, and left him there.

Quit while you're ahead, yeah?

End of term came, and I decided to go to every available party, enjoy myself and forget the whole business.

But it didn't quite work out that way, because . . .

I got home from school, and made myself a cup of tea, and I was just congratulating myself on resisting the chocolate Hobnobs, when the doorbell rang and I heard someone singing, 'We Wish You a Merry Christmas.' I groaned, fished ten pence out of my purse and went to open the door.

It was Hallo. He said, 'Will you come out on a date with me?'

I said, 'What?'

Hallo said, 'You Suze, me Hallo. We go out on date together, yes?'

I said, 'Why?'

'Because I'm fed-up with missing you,' Hallo said.

I said, 'Hallo, d'you like me or fancy me, or d'you like me more than you fancy me, or fancy me more than you like me?'

'Well I don't know, Suze!' said Hallo. 'It's just . . . when I talk to you, it makes me feel different to the way I feel when I talk to anyone else, and I'd like to find out why that is. So what d'you say? You going to give us a go?'

I stood there thinking, 'What if it goes wrong? What if I get myself into the same mess that Beth did?' Then I thought, 'But you won't. You're not Beth, and Hallo's not Craig Muir. Hallo's a nice guy, and you like him.'

And I said, 'OK.'

Hallo and I went out together and had fun, and kept on going out and having fun until Easter, when his Dad's contract ended and the family moved back to Australia. We write long, crazy letters to each other, and I know I'll see him again one day, but there's no rush. He's always going to be Hallo, and I'm always going to be me.

Jan did make friends with Tony, and we do hang out together – with Nattie and our respective boyfriends and girlfriends. There's this pub where we definitely *don't* go underage drinking on Saturday nights. Beth sometimes tags along, not very often. The scare she got over being pregnant made her more cautious about getting involved again, but I've got a sneaky feeling that might be about to change, because according to the grapevine . . .

Phone.

Downstairs, rush, rush! I pick up the receiver.

Beth's voice says, 'Guess what's happened? You'll never guess!'

But I probably can.